BLUE CHIP

A ONE EYED JACK NOVEL

By Christopher J. Lynch

BLUE CHIP

ISBN: 0-9907273-3-5

ISBN-13: 978-0-9907273-3-0

EXCEPTIONS:

Permission to use the name “Patrick Molloy’s” by management.

Permission to use the name “Raffaello Ristorante” by management.

Permission to use the name “The Kettle Restaurant” by management.

Digging Too Deep, by Jill Amadio
https://www.amazon.com/s/ref=nb_sb_noss?url=search-alias%3Daps&field-keywords=digging+toodeep+jill+amadio

SPECIAL EXCEPTIONS:

The character names Dortell Williams and Chris Moore appear in this book. They are both members of the Men For Honor Writing Group and the use of their names is with their permission, and serves as an homage to them.

Dortell Williams is the leader and facilitator of the Men For Honor Writing Group. He is a published author and an activist.

Chris Moore is a member of the group, and garnered first place in a writing contest held within the group. His winning story, *'Swept Away,'* appears at the back of this book.

ACKNOWLEDGMENTS

This book would have not have been possible without the assistance of several people:

The Men For Honor Writing Group, A-Yard, California State Prison - Los Angeles County for being some of my biggest supporters.

Dr. D. P Lyle for his expert medical opinion.

Karen Phillips, Cover Design.
http://phillipscovers.com/

Elizabeth Klug, Editor.
elizabethklug@aol.com

It is helpful to think of people as having two fundamental motivations: the desire to see ourselves as honest, good people, and the desire to gain the benefits that come from cheating—on our taxes, or on the football field.

Dan Ariely

ONE

Ever since man has competed in physical contests, he has been looking for an edge. And every once in a while, a competitor crosses the line just a little too far. From the ancient wrestler tossing sand in his opponent's eyes, to the slugger corking his bat, to deflated footballs being tossed by a quarterback in a championship game, if there is money, or fame, or ego at stake, there will always be cheaters.

Personally, I love cheaters. They are my stock and trade. I locate them, document their indiscretions, and then sell the information back to them with an easy monthly payment plan. I love cheaters because I'm a professional blackmailer.

But before you climb up onto that pedestal to preach down to me, just remember one critical fact: I have never in my career blackmailed an honest person. Like defying gravity, it just can't be done. While you chew on that tidbit of human frailty, I'll take the time to introduce myself further.

My name is John Sharp, but most people call me Jack. One Eyed Jack, to be really specific. For while I have in my possession most of my original body parts: limbs, digits, ears, nose and mouth—and most of them continue to function reasonably well—I am absent my left peeper.

This ocular deficit is courtesy one of my targets that I had, shall I say, a less than stellar business relationship with. This target eventually moved on to the great hereafter, and the henchman who orchestrated the dirty deed is MIA, but I will carry the reminder of our violent estrangement with me until the day I die. Such are the risks in a business filled with cheats, scumbags, and grifters.

*   *   *

It was a beautiful fall day in the South Bay area of Los Angeles. A fresh Santa Ana wind had blown in from the east and Raymond Chandler's dire prognostication notwithstanding, the zephyr had brought with it warm temps, a cloudless blue sky, and just a brush of a breeze. It was the kind of day that made mid-westerners and New Englanders fling their ice scrapers and scream, "Enough is enough!" People moved to Southern California because of weather like this. And when they did move, they generally moved all the way to the South Bay and to the beaches. The logic being, you came three thousand miles, why not go a couple more and really live the dream?

Many of these transplants also brought with them their loyalty to their home town football teams, and it wasn't uncommon to see ball caps, sweatshirts and bumper stickers pledging allegiance to such stalwarts of the gridiron as The Broncos, The

Steelers, or The Bears. Today, a Sunday and a game day, I would see a lot of these diehard fans when I stepped out of the bright sunshine and into Patrick Molloy's sports bar in Hermosa Beach.

The Pier Plaza in Hermosa Beach was a large open expanse that anchored the Hermosa Pier and was home to numerous dining and drinking establishments. Molloy's was one of several of the watering holes located at The Plaza, and with its attentive wait staff, great food, and reasonably priced drinks, the Irish pub/sports bar was considered a top spot to take in a game and hoist a few with some friends. I was here today to partake in neither of those revelrous activities, and instead was going to meet with one of my recent targets to discuss an alternative to his payment plan.

Like the fire triangle that you learned at summer camp or in science class, blackmailing is a triad that requires three important elements to work: a secret, the funds necessary to keep it a secret, and a guy like me who is ready, willing and able to connect the two other components together. The man I was about to meet readily possessed the first prerequisite, but he was sorely lacking in the second category. Backed into a corner, he offered up something that he swore would be more valuable to me than merely spending money every month, and so we agreed to meet.

His name was Demond Washington, and if you were to hop into a time machine and go back about a decade or so, you would have thought that he was a young man who had the world by the tail. An African American from nearby Compton, he grew up poor and fatherless, but with a God–given gift of speed and agility. Enticed by the promise of a free private education, he was recruited by the perennial football powerhouse Junipero Serra High School in Gardena where his talents were nurtured, and where he set state rushing records. His stellar performance on the field didn't escape the attention of several college scouts, and before long he was being courted by some of the top names in amateur sports. After weighing his options, he decided to stay close to home by accepting a full ride scholarship to USC. Within two years as a Trojan, he became their premiere tailback, and was in the running for the Heisman Trophy.

But with the lure of a seven figure salary dangling like a carrot in front of him, Demond—aka 'The Big D'—punted his schoolbooks into the trash at the conclusion of his sophomore year and took an early exit into pro football, where his future seemed bright. Unfortunately, the laws of physics and Mother Nature had different ideas.

The first week of training camp, Demond blew out his ACL, and he was never able to recover despite several surgeries. He was released from the team and soon found himself just one more statistic adrift in the stormy sea of washed up athletes. Uneducated, and with his prospects dim, he took various jobs until finally landing his current position: bouncer at Patrick Molloy's. That was where his real troubles began.

Her name was Karen Hays-Davidson; one of the assistant managers of Patrick Molloy's. She was twice divorced, lonely, and standing at the precipice of forty years of age. For a young buck like Demond, she was easy pickings. They became fast friends and before long it blossomed into a full blown relationship. The only wrinkle in an otherwise perfect setup was Demond's wife, who was the main breadwinner of the family, and who would toss him to the sidelines faster than a middle linebacker if she ever found out about the hanky-panky.

I stepped under the dark green awning of the outer patio of Patrick Molloy's and continued into the bar's interior. On one side of the room, a long main bar extended through nearly the length of the interior. Booths and a long, narrow two sided bar took up the remaining floor space. Like the patio area, the interior was filled to near capacity with revelers cheering on their favorite teams.

At least five different games were being shown simultaneously on upwards of twenty television monitors that encircled the room. I thought wryly that even a dragonfly with its thousands of eyes would have a difficult time keeping everything straight. But the fans didn't seem to mind, and were rabidly drinking in all the action. Many were wearing jerseys or ball caps of their favorite teams and they would high five or fist bump as their side completed a crucial pass, made a key tackle, or drove the ball down the field. I surveyed the room and noted that small banners representing each NFL team were festooned throughout the bar, but only one college team had its ensign prominently displayed at Patrick Molloy's: The University of Notre Dame. Go figure.

I grabbed one of the last open stools at the secondary bar and turned back toward the entrance. Sitting up on an elevated platform in the corner of the room was the man of the hour himself. He was dressed in a black golf shirt that had the word, 'SECURITY,' embossed above the bar's logo. From where The Big D sat, he had a bird's eye view of the entire place and could keep tabs on any patrons getting too enthusiastic.

He still appeared to be muscularly built, and his broad shoulders strained at the stitching on his short sleeved shirt. Some of the bulk may have shifted southward by now, but I wouldn't be able to determine that until he stood up.

"What can I get for you?" a waitress inquired, tossing a green and white napkin on the bar in front of me.

"Nothing yet," I said. "I'm waiting for some friends, and I want to wait until they get here to order."

"No worries," she chirped, and then bounced away to take care of other customers.

I turned back to look at Demond and thought about my rendezvous with him today. Normally speaking, I won't meet any of my targets in person, but he had insisted that he had some good info and that he didn't want to risk sending it to me via snail mail or electronic mail. I didn't feel like going back and forth about it, and I knew by checking his measly bank balance and less than stellar credit score that he was barely scraping by, so I agreed. Still, I took precautions—especially since I lived close by and didn't want to have to avoid this area for the rest of my days.

I had shaved off my normal goatee and mustache and I carried no ID, plus I wore a blond wig and sunglasses. Most importantly when it came to the art of disguise, I was wearing a fat suit along with prosthetic face and neck appliances. These were all devices used by movie industry and they could easily add about 40 pounds to an actor should a production demand it. The suit and other accoutrements were generously donated—although not without gentle coaxing by yours truly—by another target of mine. He was a special effects makeup artist in the industry and I had compromised him several years ago when I discovered he was burning and selling his SAG screeners of academy award nominated films.

I checked for secret signals being passed between Demond and any of the patrons, and seeing none, walked toward the rear of the bar and towards the restrooms. I bypassed the facilities, stepped outside behind the back of the bar and pulled out a burner smart phone that I had purchased with a prepaid credit card. I punched in Demond's number and typed in a text:

Behind bar now. Come alone or else.

I hit send and as I waited, looked around.

The backside of the bar was cluttered with all of the business items associated with catering to the needs of a thirsty clientele ready to 'party hearty.' A sturdy metal cage with propane cylinders for the patio heaters was set against the back wall, along with a string of empty beer kegs that were chained together and locked. On the wall was a painting of a Leprechaun hoisting a beer mug and advertising daily happy hours.

My phone chimed and I looked at the display. It was from a cell number that I didn't recognize, but I assumed was Demond.

A little late in the game to trying spoofing your number or changing phones pal, I thought wryly; I already know more about you than the NSA.

"K" was all the message said.

The big man himself appeared just a few moments later and stepped toward me, checking nervously to each side as he did. He had a slight limp that I'm sure was the result of his blown out knee.

He was a big man all the way around; about six foot three on a frame supporting about two hundred and sixty pounds. Most of it was dense muscle, but as I had suspected, some of his assets had already headed to lower latitudes. His head was proportional to his body, and his noggin was shaved to the skin and gleamed in the sunshine. His nose was flat, and he had large nostrils that a lazy gopher might find inviting. His ears were small and had no lobes. His dark eyes glared at me in a futile attempt to make me turn tail and run. Save your energy Big D, I thought; I've stared down tougher guys than you.

"I only got a few minutes man," he said.

His voice was higher than I thought it would have been, and was especially incongruent with his physical size.

"So do I," I shot back. "What do you have?"

"Names," he said. "Valuable names."

"Valuable how?"

"These were guys I played with."

"And…"

"And they were juicin'," Demond said.

"Juicing?"

"Steroids, growth hormones, every type of PED."

"PED's? I said.

From inside the bar a huge roar just went up as something exciting happened. Some people would be thrilled and others upset, just as money would be made and some would be lost. Sports: a zero sum game when you really broke it down.

"Performance enhancing drugs," Demond continued when the reverberations subsided. "Against all the rules, NCAA and the pros."

"Okay,' I said, pulling out my phone and hitting the record button on it. "Give 'em to me."

He looked down suspiciously at the phone like it was a pipe bomb ready to go off.

"What's that for?" he said, pointing at my phone with a finger the size of a bratwurst.

"Research," I said. "You give me the names; I'll record them and check them out."

"You ain't got to do that man."

"I'll do whatever I want to do," I shot back. "Including turning around and shooting off the video of you and your chippy going into that motel. Now quit wasting my goddamned time, Demond."

He looked from side to side, considering.

I was getting impatient with this guy, and uncomfortable; this damn suit and wig were hot. Finally, I had had enough of his waffling and turned to leave.

"Wait," he said. "K, man. I'll tell you and you can record 'em and check 'em out."

"That's better," I said. "Shoot."

In quick succession, he rattled off three names. Not being a sports junkie, the names meant nothing to me and I knew I would have to do some digging. I copied and pasted the names from the transcription of the recording into my search engine and hit, ENTER.

As I read silently through the results, Demond became even more agitated and fidgeted about. Tough luck pal, you could have sent them to me via email, but you wanted a face to face.

I looked up to him after a minute or so of torment.

"No deal," I said.

"No deal! What the fuck you mean, man? These guys were all dirty! This is valuable info!"

We both turned as the back screen door to the bar swung open. A woman leaned out of the doorway. I recognized her instantly as Karen, the Big D's slam-dance partner and the nexus of his trouble. She was dressed in a dark green shirt, black slacks, and had a towel in her hands that she used to wipe them off. She had a decent figure that might have had some work and long blond hair pulled together in a ponytail. I found her to be moderately attractive.

"Is everything okay?" she asked.

"Yeah," Demond said. "Everything's cool. I'll be back in a minute."

She eyed both of us suspiciously, but me in particular, before turning and letting the door slam closed behind her. As soon as she was gone, Demond turned back to me.

"I got to know one thing man," he said in a low voice. "Did that bitch set me up?"

I stared at him, a mixture of shock and disgust.

Nice, I thought. Between throwing your former teammates under the bus, and denigrating the women you sleep with, you missed a great opportunity running a charm school Big D.

"No," I said flatly. "You set yourself up by getting Karen pregnant and convincing her to have an abortion."

"You know about that shit man?!" he yelled.

"I know a lot of things," I replied evenly. "And I know that the names you gave me aren't worth a damn."

"What do you mean?"

I looked down at my phone and went through them one by one. The first player never even got drafted by the pros. The second one was drafted, but was cut after a single season. And the third one had been playing for three years, but he's less than a standout.

"But Terrell's still playin'!" Demond protested.

"Sure," I admitted. "But he's been traded twice, and he has bad knees. Plus he's a lineman. Even a guy like me knows that the average career at that position is only two and half seasons. NFL stands for 'Not For Long' and Terrell's days are numbered. The other guys are probably already broke, and Terrell will be in short order."

Demond looked angrily toward the ground and hissed through his teeth.

"Fuck," he said bitterly.

I waited for a few seconds and then said, “Two hundred bucks, first of every month Demond. You know where to send it.”

His meaty head turned up and he glared at me again.

“Unless you want to give me something better,” I offered.

He shifted on his feet for a moment, considering his options, which were few. Finally, he took a big inhale of breath through his nose and his large nostrils flared even larger, if that was even physically possible. They reminded me of the times in my career when I’ve stared down a double-barreled shotgun.

“Jerry Pine,” he said finally.

I pulled up my phone to type in the name.

“Forget it,” Demond said. “You won’t find him there. He doesn’t play ball.”

“So who is he then?” I asked.

“He’s the guy who gave us the juice,” Demond Washington said.

Bingo!

TWO

Another roar went up from inside the bar like someone had just scored big. I felt like I had too.

"Now we're getting somewhere," I said. "But his name won't mean shit if he's no longer the Candy Man. Is he still supplying guys?"

"I think so," Demond said absently. "Pretty sure."

Then he shifted gears, and his voice took on a more desperate tone.

"You can't let him know it was me, man" Demond insisted. "He said he'd kill any of us who snitched him out."

"Well, your wife will kill you if she ever lays eyes on the highlight reel I have of you and Karen," I countered.

"Maybe so," Demond said. "But this guy is connected. You know, mob shit."

It was a hollow threat and one that I had heard hundreds of times before. It carried about as much weight with me as the bozo who couldn't rub two nickels together who blurts out, *"You'll hear from my attorney!"*

"Sure," I said dismissively. "Everyone says they're connected, either to the mob or to Kevin Bacon. Don't worry your pretty little head about it. Give me his contact information."

"Can't. He had a cell, but the number isn't good anymore."

"How do you know?"

"Cause I tried calling him once a while back to see if he needed an assistant, you know for collections and shit. But it came back as no good. When he was supplying us, he was always changing his phone number around."

I thought about what Demond had told me and figured he was probably telling the truth. A guy in the business of supplying dope—even of the performance enhancing variety—would be smart to keep his contact info fluid, especially since he was dealing with loudmouths like the Big D. My guess was that Jerry Pine probably used a burner for a month or so before ditching it, and maybe even spoof cards.

"Do you think the coaches were ever wise to what was up with him supplying you guys?" I asked, naively.

"Hell yeah man," Demond bellowed. "They don't give a shit what you do. Like everyone else, they just want to win games. They'd just look the other way."

"What's he look like?" I asked. "This Jerry Pine?"

"Why you care what he look like man? I gave you the mother fucker's name. Check his ass out."

I remember once taking a tour of a science museum, which had a lighted display of the early incandescent light bulbs, including one of the dimmest ones ever manufactured. When I looked up at the once famous, Big "D," I couldn't help but see that dull light bulb.

"Because with only a name and no contact info, I don't have much to go on," I said. "And because maybe that's not his real name. Did you ever think that he might be a little bit brighter than you and not give you his real name?"

"Fuck you man; he wasn't that smart."

"Whatever," I said impatiently. "Give me a description. Just in case that's not his real name."

Demond shifted on his feet like he was considering whether or not to spill his guts any further. I decided to nudge him.

"It's him or you Demond," I said evenly. "You cough up a good name and a good description and you're off the hook. But if you don't…"

I let my warning hang in the air for a few moments. Then finally…

"Alright man," Demond said. "I'll give you his shit."

For the next minute or so, he gave me everything I asked for. When he was done and I was satisfied, I dropped my phone back into my pocket and turned to leave.

"Okay," I said. "I'll check him out, and if he's who you say he is and he's still in business, then you're home free."

"When will I know man?"

"As soon as I know."

I stepped away and left him standing there.

I moved across the rear parking lot and towards The Strand, which was a nice concrete path that abutted the sand and the beach. It was a gorgeous day, and I figured I might as well just stroll on home and take in the scenery.

But I had only gone a few steps when the hairs stood up on the back of my neck; something didn't feel right.

THREE

I swung back around toward Demond and saw him holding his phone and extending it out toward me. As soon as he spotted me looking at him, his dark eyes widened, and he lowered the phone and turned quickly toward the rear entrance of Patrick Molloy's, trying to act nonchalant. It didn't work.

I turned back around and continued toward The Strand, considering my options. If something was up and he was going to try to have me followed—or worse—I wanted to let it play out to see who I was dealing with.

I went past Scotty's Restaurant and stepped out onto The Strand, heading north toward Manhattan Beach and to my home. I had no intention of letting anyone tail me to my private abode, and instead hatched a quick plan.

The area was busy today with cyclists, roller bladers, skateboarders and other pedestrians, and this meant that it was too public of a place. I knew that if I was going to be followed and something was going to go down, I was going to have to allow whoever it was to get closer to me.

To aid me in my effort, I activated the rear facing video camera in a pair of specially modified Zeiss Smart Lens sunglasses I was wearing. The glasses projected the camera image into an OLED display located in the lower right corner of the inside of the lens. The glasses and their built-in camera allowed me to keep real-time tabs on anyone who was following me without having to turn around or resort to that tired old trick of looking at the reflection in storefront windows.

At the foot of The Plaza, I stepped across the faux tiled expanse, and made a beeline toward the elevated parking structure on the other side. I had only taken a few steps before I saw him projected onto the inside of my lenses.

He was a tall, well-built black man about the same age as Demond. He tipped his hand when I saw him in the display as he turned off The Strand to jog across The Plaza to catch up to me. When he was about thirty feet behind, he slowed to a sedate pace to keep his distance.

I maintained my speed and didn't give any indication that I was aware of him as I strode through the alley and toward the public parking structure.

The ground level of the structure would be busy, so I climbed the steps to the second floor of the structure where I figured my tail would feel comfortable about confronting me. I noticed that he dropped back a bit to put a little more distance between us, but I also knew that he would make it up rapidly as soon as it was safe to do so.

When I got to the second floor I was happy to see that nobody was getting in or out of their cars, or waiting for a spot to open up. But between the games and the nice weather, I knew that it was a busy day at the beach and that the solitude wouldn't last for long. My newfound friend probably knew this as well, and if he was going to make a move, it would have to be quick.

I had a suppressed Berreta M9A3 in a holster under the suit, but I didn't want to resort to lethal countermeasures unless I really needed to. Instead, I reached into the pocket of my pants and pulled out a ring of keys. On the ring was a singular key that looked like a standard automotive key. It was anything but, and had been designed for foreign operatives by the CIA.

I reached down and removed a carefully crafted sheath that resembled the grooves and lands of a key. Underneath the sheath was a small thin blade that had a tiny hole drilled through it all the way to the bow of the key. With the sheath removed, the bow of the key could be squeezed to force liquid through to the blade tip. Essentially, it was a knife/syringe masquerading as a car key, and The Big D's buddy just might get himself a free immunization today.

By now, my tail had closed the distance between us to about ten feet. I maintained the illusion of ignorance and turned between two parked cars. That did it; he made his move. On the display I saw a steel pipe come out.

Realizing that like most street attackers, he would aim high and attempt to go for my skull, so I dropped down into a crouching position just as he swung down.

His swing missed me with a foot to spare, and his forward momentum caused him to lose his balance and fall onto me. This put his lower body even with my head and I spun quickly and jammed the key blade through his pants and into his left quadriceps.

"Aaagh!" he screamed. "Mother fucker!"

As soon as I felt the blade bury into the thick muscle, I squeezed the bow of the key and emptied the contents into him. My toxin of choice was a diluted form of Etorphine (M99), a strong opioid normally used to tranquilize elephants and other large mammals. It was fast-acting, had few side effects, and unlike paralytic drugs, didn't stop the recipient's breathing functions. I had just the right potency and amount to put this guy down for a few minutes, provided he couldn't get up in time to get another swing at me.

He was squirming and I felt his bulk on me as he struggled to regain his footing. But the dope was already kicking in, and I felt—rather than saw—his body go limp. In a matter of seconds, he was nothing more than a lifeless mass of flesh, bone and muscle on top of me.

I rolled out from under him and he went straight to the ground, his body like a sack of potatoes.

I took a quick look around the parking structure to make sure no one was coming, and then reached into his pants pocket. I found his phone, and pulled it out to look at it. The image taken by Demond of my backside was still up on the device's display.

"Not too bright Big D," I said aloud. "Especially if your former candy man is worth anything."

Not wanting my attacker to asphyxiate if he vomited, I rolled him onto his side, and pushed his back up against one of the cars. He had already wet himself, and a long string of drool was coming out of the corner of his mouth. Sleep well pal.

I stepped away, and began heading out of the structure. Then I thought better of it, and went back to the scene of the crime.

I snapped a quick picture of him using his own phone and then went to the phone's contact list. I found Demond's mobile number, as well as a hundred or so others. I tapped the 'SELECT ALL' soft key on the display and then sent the image to everyone who knew this guy. When he finally came to, he would have a lot of people asking him why they received a picture of him looking like a passed out, drunken sailor. A lesson here to any of my targets that might be entertaining the thought of messing with me; I happen to consider life very precious—especially if it's my own. Think of this as your courtesy warning.

After I was sure the picture had been sent, I removed the battery from the phone so that it couldn't be traced, and tucked them both into my pocket.

I walked down the steps of the parking structure, and when I hit grade level, pulled out my own burner. Now it was time to deal with the instigator of this whole sordid mess.

There are times in my business when a target simply becomes far more trouble than they were worth. Between his precarious finances, my acrimonious meeting with him, and the failed attack that he had just orchestrated, the Big D had just earned himself this dubious honor. Besides that, he already coughed up a possible gold mine of information for me with the name of his steroid supplier.

I pulled up the video of Demond and Karen visiting the good old 'No Tell Mo-Tel' and sent the link to Demond's wife, as well as to all of her family and her friends.

As soon as it was sent, I slipped the phone back into my pocket and turned north onto The Strand to head home. Before long, I found myself humming the Notre Dame fight song as I walked along.

It really was a great day in Southern California.

FOUR

I arrived home, several long and painful minutes later. I was sweating profusely from both the fat suit and the prosthetics, and quickly stripped the suit off as soon as I stepped through the door.

Home was a three-story, five bedroom house located directly on The Strand in Manhattan Beach. It had stunning ocean views, a gourmet kitchen, six fireplaces and an elevator. The current value was just over eight million, and it was more home than I could ever need or ever thought I could afford. It also came to me—or rather to my girlfriend, Tiffany and myself—in a rather serendipitous fashion.

While teaming up to dig into her late husband's life and finances, we happened to discover a substantial cache of extremely precious gems squirreled away in an old storage facility he had rented. The gems, I suspected, had been stolen, and possibly used as payment to Tiffany's husband, who had performed identity altering plastic surgery on a Russian mobster on the lam.

Realizing what we had stumbled upon, I fenced the stones through several crooked gemologists I knew dealt in this sort of thing, and then funneled the money through to an offshore corporation that we used to buy the home.

Besides the home, the fact that Tiffany and I ever became acquainted or ended up in an intimate relationship was a fluke in itself. After all, it was her late husband who removed my left eye.

I dumped the fat suit into the clothes hamper in the utility room, and climbed the stairs up to the third floor and to our bedroom and master bath. In the bathroom, I applied surgical spirits to dissolve the adhesives used to fuse the prosthetics onto my face. I also checked for cuts, scrapes or any sort of injuries.

In a fight, things happen quickly and the adrenaline is really pumping. In plenty of cases, people are not aware of any injuries—including knife wounds—they might have sustained, until much later.

Not looking any worse for wear, I took a quick shower, threw on an old pair of cargo shorts and a T-shirt and headed into my office. Tiffany was out shopping with a girlfriend and I figured I could get in a couple hours of work before she returned.

While steroid and PED use had long been considered to be associated with increased muscular/skeletal injuries in players, now a growing number of researchers were finding a connection between it and traumatic brain injuries, so called CTE, or Chronic Traumatic Encephalopathy. The suicides of high profile players such as Junior Seau and Dave Duerson, who were later diagnosed to have suffered with CTE, helped to thrust the issue—and an accompanying lawsuit—to the forefront of the debate.

As a result, the NCAA had upped their penalties for a first offense in the use of such performance enhancers from one season to two seasons of ineligibility, with a lifelong suspension for a second offense.

Piggybacking on to the NCAA ruling, the new NFL commissioner had instituted a far more intrusive and aggressive testing program and instituted a zero tolerance policy with a lifetime ban for any player being caught using the drugs. On top of that, any college player that had been found to have used PEDs or steroids during his college years would be ineligible to enter the NFL draft. The bottom line: the downside for college and professional football players getting caught juicing had never been more detrimental. And therefore, the upside for me knowing about them doing so had never been so good.

Now I just had to learn everything there was to know about Mr. Jerry Pine, aka “Juice-Man.”

Back in my office, the first thing I did was log onto the Emperium website. Emperium was a service used by private investigators, journalists, and law enforcement professionals, and could dig up just about any information on individuals from tax records to medical reports, arrest records, as well as a host of other private information. I had used the service extensively in my former job as an insurance fraud investigator and found it to be a great tool.

How I happened to still retain access to the site was courtesy of my former supervisor who tried to sabotage my career in order to keep the spotlight focused strictly on her. When I found out about her nefarious machinations, I turned the tables on her and resorted to my old blackmailing tricks. I didn't take long before I uncovered some dirt, and found out about a little hanky-panky that was going on between her and a man our company was investigating. Presented with the evidence, and knowing that it was a terminable offense, she wisely agreed to allow me to retire with a nice severance package while still retaining usage of the service. And I haven't looked back since.

I typed in the name Jerry Pine along with any location within a one hundred mile radius of both Los Angeles and San Diego. I knew that many of the drugs supplied to athletes and bodybuilders came from Mexico via Tijuana, and I didn't want to leave any stone unturned.

The search returned seventeen hits, but before I began to methodically sift through them, I launched another program. It was an image building tool used by police departments when putting together a composite "sketch" of a suspect based on witness descriptions. Using handy pull-down menus for such things as gender, age, race, hairstyle, eye color, etc, I put together my best guess of what the Juice-Man looked like based on Demond's description.

Only four of the seventeen initial hits came close to my rendition, mostly based on age and eye and hair color, but none really seemed to jump out at me.

I studied the faces, wondering if I was just wasting my time. After all, what does a steroid dealer look like anyway? Or for that matter, what about an embezzler, or a bank-robber, or a pedophile? Can we really judge a book by its cover? Was I the image of the prototypical blackmailer?

Still, it was all I had at this point and so I soldiered on, switching tactics to begin looking into other aspects of each of my Jerry Pine candidates to see if I could uncover any telltale signs. The most glaring of these was often a lopsided standard of living relative to income.

Out of the four possible Jerry Pines I had come up with, all seemed to have a lifestyle in line with their income levels except for one. I decided to call him *Jerry 1*, and I numbered the others, *Jerry 2, 3, and 4,* and saved their dossiers to be revisited later.

Jerry Pine 1 lived in a very large home in the coastal town of Dana Point, a pricey enclave located about halfway between San Diego and Los Angeles. This close proximity to the border would have made trips to Mexico to pick up the PEDs convenient. That fact notwithstanding, what really set off the alarm bells though was his profession. He worked as a real estate appraiser in the area, which was an honest job that generated modest income. But in order to inhabit such fancy digs, Jerry numero uno would have needed substantial supplementary income.

It would have been easy to smell a rat and blurt out; “Ah-ha!” but people’s lives were rarely as simple and straightforward as they appeared on the surface. I looked into his marital status and found out that he was in fact married, as well as his wife's current profession. And that was where I hit pay dirt, or a dead end, depending on how you looked at it.

Meredith Pine, aka Mrs. Jerry Pine, was a real estate broker. But not just any broker. She had a thriving business and was probably one of the top sellers of properties in the Newport Beach and Dana Point area. Her website listed such recently closed deals as a Balboa Bay dockside three bedroom, three bath home for a measly $4.2 million and a thirteen thousand square foot mansion overlooking the Pacific Ocean for $40 million. Her office currently had listings that if they closed even close to the asking price, could easily be worth over $10 million in commissions. Lucky man, that Jerry Pine. He got to drive around, gawk at a few properties, and then come home to a pad that might have been featured on the show, *Lifestyles of the Rich and Famous.*

I pulled up his original picture again and stared at it. He was a nice looking man with graying hair and a smile that said he hadn't a care in the world.

"Would you really risk giving up the *Life of Riley* by pushing some pills to some meathead linebacker Jerry?" I asked.

Not likely, I thought, and saved and closed the file.

I leaned back in my chair and stretched my arms across the desk. I looked back at the computer screen and wondered if I should continue. None of these Jerry Pines could be Demond's Jerry, or any one of them could be. The other very real possibility was that Demond had been sold a bill of goods and the real perpetrator was not named Jerry Pine. He could be Jack Pine, Gerald Pine. Jerry Piner, or any one of a number of possible iterations. It was like watching Johnny Carson do his old *Tea-Time Flick* gag and reciting a gaggle of interrelated names.

I opened a special program I had that could take names and generate aliases based upon the root name. I typed in Jerry Pine, adjusted the relevance setting to medium and hit enter.

The program immediately generated twenty-two possible aliases, some of which had occurred to me naturally, and some I hadn't even thought of. I shook my head, knowing what a Pandora's Box I had opened. With this many possible name combinations, I would probably have to check over five hundred IDs.

I had successfully dealt with this volume of research previously, but Demond's case just had too many question marks in it. What was the dealer's real name? Was he still juicing athletes? Or even, did Demond just concoct the whole thing to get me off his back? If he was capable of ordering a hit on me, then plain old deception certainly didn't seem out of the realm of possibilities.

That last thought did it.

Being in a mood that was growing pissier by the moment, I did what a lot of people did when they felt ticked off; I paid it back in spades by hurting someone else.

I pulled out my attacker's phone, reinstalled the battery and hooked it up to my computer.

My good friend and hacker extraordinaire Zahid Shukla had given me a copy of a very devious program he had developed. I had Demond's home address and with Zahid's software, I could reprogram the attacker's phone GPS to show that it was located there. If the guy had the "Find My Phone" app and searched for it online, the location would track back to Demond's house. The attacker would show up there demanding to get his property back, which the former football star didn't possess, and the fur would fly. It's often quipped that 'There is no honor among thieves.' In a short time, there would be no harmony as well. Have fun playing in the sandbox boys.

Feeling somewhat sated now that the wheels of revenge had been put into motion, I returned to my task at hand. There had to be a smarter way to go about finding the Juice-man—but should I even waste my time? How much was all of this work going to net me?

I stood up from my desk and walked over to the window that faced the ocean to ponder my situation and determine the best course of action.

Besides the wildfires that they helped to cultivate, the other downside to a strong Santa Ana wind was the fact that it pushed all of LA's smog out west over the Pacific. This action made the skies above the LA area clear, but a sickly mocha colored band of pollution would stretch from horizon to horizon over the water.

The brown band was there, and the sun was now slowly starting to disappear into it. As usual, time had slipped away from me while I was busy at work and soon it would be getting dark. It was also getting close to dinner, and I had promised to concoct the feast tonight.

FIVE

Since I had been on my own as soon as I could move away from my dad and stepmom, I had learned to fend for myself, and these survival skills extended to the kitchen as well. I genuinely enjoyed cooking and through the years had amassed quite a collection of favorite recipes. The dishes ran from the simple to the exotic, but all were tasty and just as important, were fun to prepare.

This evening's entrée was an easy to prepare yet delicious, chicken pesto pasta. It was not only great tasting, if you multitasked, it could be made in about thirty minutes flat.

Thinking it might be a prudent thing to do with my new foray into the world of sports, as well as keeping me company while I cooked, I switched on the TV in the kitchen to search for a football game.

I quickly found a game on one of the satellite sports channels. Voice-over from the announcer and the color man were going back and forth about a player's yards per carry, matchups with defenders, and so forth just as a huge running back deftly broke through a couple of tackles, and returned the ball fifty-three yards for an uncontested touchdown. A roar went up from the crowd and within seconds, the instant replay was on and the announcers were analyzing every nuance of the player's moves.

While they were droning on in the background, I set out a two quart and a four quart stainless steel pot, and got to work. I filled the smaller of the two pots halfway with water and set to boil. In the four quart pot, I splashed in a couple of teaspoons of olive oil and turned the heat to medium. As the oil was heating, I cleaned and sliced two boneless chicken breasts lengthwise so that they were only a half inch thick.

This task accomplished, I dropped the breasts into the hot oil and checked on the water for the pasta, which was still not boiling as a properly watched pot should behave.

As this was going on, I pulled out the food processor from its garage at the end of the counter and dropped in a couple peeled garlic cloves after switching the unit on. The cloves danced and flew around on the rapidly spinning blades and after a couple of scrapes and resets; I had a nice amount of freshly minced garlic.

I checked on the chicken and realized it had a few more minutes to go on the first side. As luck would have it though, the water was boiling, so I dropped in a package of cheese tortellini, setting the clock for eight minutes.

I returned to the food processor, and added in the remaining ingredients: two tablespoons of pine nuts, a half cup of grated parmesan, a half cup of olive oil, and four cups of loosely packed basil.

I switched the unit on and watched as it quickly transformed the raw ingredients into the creamy pale green mixture. Mmmmm.

The chicken was done on one side, so I flipped it over and figured it would take about as long as the boiling pasta to finish.

With nothing to do as the chicken and the pasta continued to cook, I pulled out a wineglass and poured myself some chilled Sauvignon Blanc. I took a sip and savored the sweet flavor.

"Smells great Jack," I heard from behind me.

I turned to the sound to see Tiffany standing in the entrance to the kitchen. In her hands hung several bags from high-end department stores, as well as one from *Victoria's Secret*.

She was dressed in a pair of snug fitting jeans and a white boat neck tee with three-quarter sleeves. One side of her long blond hair cascaded down the front. She was an incredibly beautiful woman with a great figure, high cheekbones, and beautiful emerald green eyes. Staring at her, I marveled that she could look equally sexy in a black evening gown, or an old pair of sweatpants. With a depth of beauty like hers, it just didn't matter. I really was a lucky guy.

"Hi beautiful," I said. "How was the shopping?"

"Fun," she said, setting the bags down on the counter top.

We embraced and shared a nice kiss.

"Would you like a glass of wine?" I offered.

"Love one," she said.

I poured her a glass and we toasted before taking sips.

"What are you making?" she asked, her nostrils taking in the scent.

"Chicken pesto pasta."

"It smells wonderful," she said approvingly. "Just like the old country, that is, if I knew what the old country smelled like. Ha, ha."

Hearing Tiffany's statement triggered something in me; I had an idea about what to do about the Jerry Pine conundrum. I set my wineglass down.

"Just a second baby," I said, pulling out my phone. "You just made me think of something. I need to make a phone call."

"Sure," she said easily. "I'm going to run this stuff upstairs. Then maybe later I can give you a little fashion show."

She ended the sentence with a little wink and disappeared out of the kitchen.

I speed dialed a number in my phone and it was answered a short time later by a coarse, gravelly voice that was none the less, music to my ears.

"Jack," the grating voice bellowed. "One—Fucking—Eyed—Jack. To what do I owe this pleasure?"

His name was Tony Scarcetti, aka 'Big Tony' Scarcetti. He was a highly successful bookie and loan shark in the Los Angeles and Orange County areas. When it came to sports and betting, be it horses, basketball games, boxing matches—or most importantly, football—he seemed to have a line on everything and everyone associated with it. Listening through the phone in the background I could hear one of the games blasting from a TV and I wondered why I hadn't just gone to him first.

"I need some information Tony," I said. "But I don't want to disturb you. Is this a bad time to talk?"

"Nah. Don't worry about it Jack. If you had called about an hour ago though, it would have been really bad."

The statement piqued my curiosity, and I said, "Oh?"

"Yeah, I was getting a blow job."

He started to laugh a big hearty laugh at his own joke, and before long this triggered a full-blown coughing jag. Tony had been smoking since he was a young boy growing up in Sicily and he currently burned through at least four packs a day. It was painful to listen to.

When the hacking fit subsided, he said, "Okay, Jack. So what info do you want?"

"Does the name Jerry Pine mean anything to you?" I asked.

"No. Should it? Does he owe me money?"

"Not sure," I said. "But he might make or lose lots of money for you or for others in your business."

"Now you got my attention Jack," his hoarse voice said. "How about lunch tomorrow?"

"Sure I said. When and where?"

"Raffaello Ristorante in San Pedro. It's the best."

I put Tony on speaker and pulled up the restaurant on my phone.

"That's the one on Pacific and Fourth, right?"

I heard Tony's raw bark emanate from the speaker of my phone. "Yeah. Meet me there at three for lunch."

I did a double take and looked at the display on my phone. The restaurant's contact info and hours were displayed on it.

"But they're closed until five Tony," I said.

"Not for me they're not, Jack. Three o'clock, tomorrow."

Then he hung up.

I terminated the call, and looked up to find Tiffany standing in the entrance to the kitchen. Her lithe body was angled seductively against the doorframe.

"So how about that little fashion show," she purred. "Or maybe, something even more?"

I tossed my phone down on the counter and smiled.

"I'll take the more," I said.

SIX

I arrived at Raffaello Ristorante a few minutes before three and pulled into the back lot. Tony's shiny black CTS-V Cadillac sedan was already parked there.

The exterior of the restaurant was fairly nondescript, but still tastefully done. The front/street side consisted of a facade of faux arches interspersed with tall Boxwood hedges. The walls were plaster, and the colors were beige with brown accents. Muted as the building was, if you weren't looking for it, you might go right past.

Still, as Tony had stated unequivocally, the establishment was considered one of best Italian eateries in town of San Pedro, a working class community of roughly eighty-thousand located at the eastern end of the Palos Verdes Peninsula. The town has the distinction of having the largest Italian American population in Southern California; many of whom were lured to the area by its Mediterranean climate and its familiar feel to their native homeland.

I walked to the back door and knocked a couple of times. A few moments later I heard the sound of some footsteps coming from the other side of the door. A young Hispanic man in a tomato sauce stained apron cautiously cracked the door open a few inches.

"Jack a conocer a Tony," I said in Spanish.

The man nodded and closed the door. I could hear some muffled conversation in Spanish coming from behind it, and then the door opened wide.

"Entrar," another Hispanic man said, and I stepped through the doorway. He led me through the kitchen, past several other workers, who were either washing dishes or chopping vegetables.

We stepped out of the kitchen and past a semi-circular cherry wood bar that was laden with wine bottles of all types and vintages. A gravelly voice called out from the main dining room.

"Over here Jack."

I turned toward the sound and continued on into the main room. It was a large area, about thirty by thirty, and the interior was done up in the same soft beige and brown colors as the exterior. The walls were done in wood panels inset with tall rectangular windows with textured glass that gave the impression of rain sheeting down. Large framed oil paintings of "The Old Country" were mounted here and there and sconce lights, with their glow muted, cast wedge shaped shadows up the walls. A coffered ceiling with hammered tin panels completed the room. It was all very warm and cozy, and it was easy to see why the restaurant was a favorite of locals and visitors alike.

I moved over to a large square table of inlaid wood and took a seat across from Tony. He shifted a lighted cigarette out of his right hand into his left and proffered a meaty paw for me to shake.

"How ya doing, Jack?"

"Great, Tony. Never better. How about you?"

He shifted the cigarette back into his right hand and took a long drag, blowing the smoke toward the ceiling as he exhaled. On the table in front of him was an ashtray with five crushed butts in it.

"Can't complain. Nobody listens anyway."

I smiled at the self-deprecating humor and took a good look at him.

Never small of statue, he had gained even more weight since I last saw him, and was now easily north of three hundred pounds. He was wearing a long sleeve white dress shirt and black slacks. His shirt was opened at the top and a tangled mass of salt and pepper chest hair poked out of it. He had a massive square head about the size of an engine block supported by at least three chins and a thick stump that passed for a neck. His hair was thick, slicked back and was dyed the color of black shoe polish. I could spy some gray roots at the base of the oily follicles. His eyes were dark and hard, and he had a large bulbous nose the color of a flamingo.

He reached for a bottle of 2010 Argiano Solengo that was on the table and poured a glass for me.

"Here Jack, have some wine."

I took the glass as Tony topped off his own, and we raised them together.

"Per cent'anni!" I said.

"And to you too, Jack."

I took a sip of my wine and it was like an express trip to heaven. Tony never skimped when it came to women, food or drink, and I wouldn't be surprised if these squished grapes cost at least two hundred bucks a bottle.

A man appeared at the side of our table and set out two plates, along with a bowl of roasted peppers sautéed in garlic and olive oil.

Tony placed one of his big hands on the man's shoulder and said, "Gino, I'd like you to meet my good friend, Jack. Gino's the owner here and he'll take good care of you. Anything he wants Gino, okay?"

Gino took my hand and shook it enthusiastically. It was warm like he had just taken it out of a basket of freshly baked bread.

"Of course," he said. "Buona giornata!"

"Buona giornata!" I replied.

He moved off and Tony began to shovel heaping spoons of the roasted peppers onto his plate. I followed suit and then grabbed a slice of garlic bread.

I took a fork full of peppers into my mouth and followed it with a bite of garlic bread dredged in the olive oil. It was delicious.

I picked up my wineglass to wash it down and as I was sipping, Tony spoke up, talking between bites.

"So tell me about this guy you mentioned yesterday, Jack. What was his name? Jerry something?"

"Jerry Pine," I said. "He's supposedly a juicer—college athletes. Supplies them with all the dope they need to hopefully make it to the prime time. I'm trying to get a line on him."

Tony took a big swallow of wine, and then followed it with a drag on his cigarette.

“Where’d ya get the name?” he asked, blowing a cloud of bluish smoke sideways out of the corner of his mouth.

“Guy I was leaning on for screwing around on his wife. He was a one time pro football player until his knee went south on him. He claimed he didn’t have the bank to pay me—and he didn’t—and so he tried offering up the names of some of his old teammates in college that had been doing steroids and PEDs. I guess he figured that if I could get more out of them than him, he would be off the hook.”

“Sounds thin.”

“It was. These guys weren’t worth a shit and I told him so. He was desperate and so he gave up the dealer’s name. Claims he’s connected.”

Tony’s big head cocked to the side and his eyes narrowed.

“Is that so?”

“So he says. You ever heard of the guy?”

Tony shook a cigarette out of a pack on the table in front of him and put it in his mouth. He used the cherry on the nearly finished one to light it. He once bragged to me that he only used one match a day to light his first cigarette, and that he lit all of the rest off of the original one. Resourceful, and ecologically friendly.

"If that's his real name, then I'm calling bullshit on your friend, Jack" he said. "If he was a part of the life, I'd know about him."

"That's what I figured."

I took another bite of peppers and washed them down with some more wine.

"So do you know how I could find this guy, Tony? I've tried my usual methods, and so far haven't gotten any traction."

Just then, a couple of men stepped into the opening to the room. Both were in their late twenties or early thirties. Both were tall, muscular and menacing looking. One of the men, his huge biceps straining at the seams of his short sleeved shirt, was carrying a brown paper bag in one of his hands. He stopped in his tracks when he saw me and looked cautiously at Tony.

Tony caught his hesitation and said, “C’mon in, Angelo. This is Jack. He’s alright.”

“Sorry to interrupt Tony,” the man said apologetically.

Tony waved a big hand dismissively and said, “Don’t worry about it. What’cha got?”

Angelo reached into the bag and pulled out a stack of currency about two inches thick and bound with a rubber band. He set it on the table. Tony looked at it and grabbed one end, thumbing the stack. It sounded like playing cards in bicycle spokes. Based on the denominations and the amount, I guessed it to be close to three grand.

“It feels light,” Tony said. “Nichols again?”

Angelo nodded. “Yeah, says he forgot.”

“Remind him,” Tony barked.

“Got it,” Angelo said. He smiled hungrily, a single gold tooth in the front of his mouth. I could almost hear bones breaking. He turned and walked away, leaving the wad of bills still on the table.

“Fucking guys,” Tony lamented. “They make all this money working on the docks, try to triple it with the ponies, and then when they overextend themselves, it's my problem."

I nodded sympathetically. With the Port of Los Angeles being a big employer in the city of San Pedro, Tony did a brisk business with the longshoreman who worked the container ships. They made great money, but more times than not, were less than savvy in their management of it.

"So where were we Jack?" Tony said. "Oh yeah, your juice guy. So you're hoping to score some major scratch by leaning on him, am I right?"

"Right."

The big man took another puff on his cigarette, and stared over the top of it at me. As he expelled the smoke skyward he said, "You'll never do it, Jack."

I was stunned by the assertion. "What do you mean, Tony?"

He set his cigarette in the ashtray.

"What I mean," he said. "Is that you're going about this the wrong way. You need to back into this one."

"I'm listening," I said.

"Alright. Let's say for sake of argument that this guy is still supplying dope to the players, which may or may not be the case. He could have gotten tired of it and moved on already."

"True," I said.

"But, if he is, *and* you can locate him, *and* you can get the goods on him, just how much do think you can get out of this guy, Jack?"

"Maybe not a lot," I admitted. "But I was hoping to get the names of all of the guys he was supplying."

"That's what I thought, but then what, Jack?" Tony asked. "These kids playing in college don't have any money, not until they make it to the big time. And there's no guarantee any of the lunks he's supplying will make it there. You could be waiting a long time, and monitoring a whole bunch of guys for nothing."

I pondered Tony's statement. He was certainly correct that just because a player is doping to gain an edge that it might not be enough to carry him to the pros. The odds were certainly against it. There were over three hundred and fifty million people in the US, and less than two thousand played professional football.

“So what do you suggest, Tony?” I asked.

“You need to go where the highest percentage of prospects are,” he said. “That’s where you’ll find your future draft picks, your blue chips, and you focus on them.”

“And you know where that would be? I stated, as much as asked.

“Yeah, I know of a place,” he said.

He grabbed his cigarette and took a puff. It was almost done, and he shook a fresh lung dart out of his pack.

“UCLB,” he said, as he went through the same efficient ritual to light his new cigarette. “Right across the harbor in Long Beach.”

“They have a lot of potential NFL players?”

“"Yeah,” Tony growled, as smoke drifted out of his mouth. “Too many to be a coincidence. Especially one of them.”

“Who’s that?”

“The bluest of the blue chips himself,” Tony Scarcetti said. “Dortell Williams.”

SEVEN

Always in the shadow of its bigger brother UCLA, the University of California at Long Beach (UCLB) had none the less clawed its way through the competitive arena of higher education to become a top notch university and one who's academic—and now athletic—reputation could not be ignored. Enrollment had climbed steadily since the campus opened in 1982, and it had one of the premiere engineering schools in the nation as well as a cutting-edge biotechnology department. The university was the recipient of numerous awards, and with this came grants, endowments, and the undying support of its alumni.

After finishing lunch with Tony, I thanked him for his advice and headed over to the campus to see if I could locate his blue chip player, the young phenom by the name of Dortell Williams.

The city of Long Beach was located on the other side of several shipping ports that separated it from the town of San Pedro, so I took a ride over the Vincent Thomas Bridge, a giant arch of green painted steel, to the UCLB campus.

As I headed over the bridge, the world class Port of Los Angeles was below me. Rows of enormous hammerhead cranes stood ready to offload the giant ships laden with cargo containers, as forklifts buzzed around dockside. One of San Pedro's top tourist attractions, the Battleship Iowa stood off in the distance, and a giant, white cruise ship, probably heading down to Mexico, passed under me as I crested the top of the bridge.

As I drove, I listened to a replay of a *Sports Center* broadcast where the two hosts discussed Dortell Williams. He was a local African American kid from nearby Compton, who had played at Centennial High School. He played tight end and fullback and was an average player his freshman year and halfway through his sophomore year. He had to sit out the second half of the season when an illness kept him out for the remainder of the year. Most everyone—including Dortell himself—thought that he would never be able to return to the gridiron, but he proved the naysayers wrong when he showed up to summer practice and promptly blew everyone away.

"The kid just blossomed in the time he was off," one of his high school coaches would recall. "I've seen it happen with kids before, but never to this degree."

Dortell easily made the varsity team his junior year and was moved to the half back position where he became a starter. His standout performances kept him in the spotlight, and in the crosshairs of several universities looking to court him with a full ride scholarship. He settled on UCLB and was a starter his freshman year. He was currently a sophomore and the speculation was that he was planning on renouncing his remaining NCAA eligibility at the end of the season to take an early entry into the NFL draft. In short, he was a young man whose future seemed very bright, and for me, very profitable.

I arrived at UCLB about a half an hour later, parked my car, and after getting my bearings, headed across campus to football stadium. The school was clean, open, and energy and resource efficient, having garnered the prestigious rank of Platinum LEED, or Leadership in Energy and Environmental Design certification. Sleek, glass front buildings sat at odd angles to one another, with tall eucalyptus trees punctuating the space between them. Here and there, students lounged on the expansive green spaces listening to music or reading. Others had more pressing schedules to keep, and moved briskly to get to their classes. Some of them were on skateboards and they deftly knifed through the crowds as they scooted along. A lot had changed since I attended school, and I suddenly felt very old and out of touch.

Before I left him, Tony had warned me that the practices would most likely be closed to the public and that I couldn't get in without a press pass. But I had to remind him of who he was talking to.

A year or so ago, I got a line on a phony company that was taking tobacco lawsuit settlement money and funneling it to dubious pet projects for city officials. The scam was nothing new to me, and I knew that I had hit some good pay dirt with all the principles involved, but one of them took me by surprise. He was the editor of a Los Angeles newspaper who had uncovered pretty much the same info I had, but he was going to bury the story after taking a huge bribe from the company in exchange for his silence. I braced him about it and he knew that I had him smoked. Besides the money I collected from him every month in exchange for my silence, I also enjoyed perks such as press passes.

A tall chain link fence created a perimeter barrier between the football stadium and the rest of the campus. A single gate was propped open, and a young security guard in black slacks and a white shirt stood by watching the entrance and checking IDs. With the phony pass hanging over my neck on a lanyard, I walked up to the guard like I had done this a million times before.

Besides looking like it was routine, I knew that to play the role to the hilt, I also had to look bored and disappointed in my current station in life. I was just one more hack sports writer for a mid-level newspaper who hadn't won the Pulitzer, or had a NY Times bestseller to my credit.

I held up the badge for the guard to see as I passed through and noticed that he barely looked at it. Heck, he was even more bored and disenchanted than I was.

Inside the wire, I circled around the side of the stadium to where I noticed a bunch of other reporters milling about outside the entrance to the locker room. As I expected, practice was over for the day, but I knew that there was better gold to mine by getting into the locker room and talking to the players.

The door to the locker room was closed, and I deduced that some sort of a team meeting was taking place inside. Some of the reporters were jotting down notes on little pads, while others stayed busy checking their phones. Most looked as bored as the image I tried to project. Above the locker room door was a huge painted logo of the school's mascot, a fierce looking dolphin with the nickname of "Dominic."

"I wish they wouldn't stroke these damn team meetings out so long," I heard a nearby voice say. "I've got a tight deadline and my editor's going to ream me if I'm late again."

I hadn't noticed, but another reporter had drifted toward me. He was a light skinned African American of slight stature. He was nattily attired in beige slacks and had on a white long sleeve dress shirt with a blue tie with tiny white stars on it. His hair was closely cropped and he wore glasses.

"I know what you mean," I said sympathetically.

He stuck out his hand and we shook.

"Chris Moore, Los Angles Chronicle," he said.

"Jack Roberts," I said.

Chris looked over and read my press pass. His dark brown eyes were very intense.

"LA Post," he said curiously. "I didn't think you guys covered the beat and just got your stuff off the wire?"

"New management, new direction," I said with a shrug.

Chris snorted, "You're telling me," he said derisively. "Change for the sake of change."

The door to the locker room swung open and a staff member pushed it into the locked position. The herd of reporters started to drive toward the entrance. Soon a small cluster had clogged the doorway and Chris and I were caught shoulder to shoulder against each other.

"I never heard of you before," he said. "Are you new?"

"Yeah," I said. "Moved from Chicago. I was with the Tribune."

He looked at me, startled.

"You left the Tribune to come work for the LA Post?" he said incredulously.

I looked back at him and chuckled.

"Yeah," I said. "You ever have to shovel two feet of snow off your car just to get to work?"

Chris held up his hands in mock surrender and said, smiling, "You got me there Jack."

The mob finally squeezed its way through the entrance, and we went down a short hall and into the locker room.

It was a large, square room at least fifty feet long on each side and carpeted wall to wall with the teal and gray colors of the school. Another logo of Dominic the Dolphin was printed into the carpeting. In lieu of metal lockers for equipment and uniforms, cubbyholes, like large, open wardrobes, lined the walls with each player designated a certain space. The room was crowded with coaches, trainers, and players in various stages of undress. Some had already stripped down to their pants, while others still had their shoulder pads on. The place was boisterous, and smelled of disinfectant, sweat, and testosterone.

Even though Tony had given me the name of Dortell and several other premiere players he thought I should investigate, other than seeing a picture of Dortell, I didn't know any of the others by sight. I thought that it might be suspicious if I started asking who was who, or began nosing around trying to read the nametags above each cubby, so instead, I peeled off from my newfound friend and strolled over to where several reporters were huddled around a player.

The name above his space read ‘Kowalski’, and I figured he was probably Ted Kowalski, a middle linebacker, and one of the players Tony had mentioned as promising—and probably dirty. He was a huge white kid who was three hundred pounds if he was an ounce. Besides his suspiciously massive girth, he had the thinning hair and pimples that characterized someone who was juicing on steroids. To fit in with the other reporters, I pulled out a notepad and began scribbling in it as questions were being fired at him.

“How do you think the four-four is going to work against the Cardinals passing game?”

“You bounce from the middle to strong-side linebacker a lot. Which one do you prefer to play?”

“Do you anticipate the blitz being an important factor in Saturday’s game?”

Kowalski handled the barrage of inquiries professionally, albeit with a satisfied grin on his face. He was a young man who was going places, and he enjoyed the attention he was getting right now.

Out of the corner of my eye, I saw a larger group of reporters including Chris, clustered around another player who I recognized as Dortell. I acted like I had gotten all that I needed from the incredible hulk, and moved over to Dortell.

Dortell was a large man, but not freakishly so like Kowalski. His skin was clear, and he had a nice crop of short hair that didn't show any signs of thinning. Interesting, and I wondered if African Americans exhibited the same telltale signs of steroid use as white players.

The exchange between Dortell and the reporters was a general replay of the same drill with the linebacker and he was peppered with questions, which he fielded nicely. I continued my sham of jotting down notes, but since I didn't want to blow my cover by showing my ignorance of the sport, never fired off any questions of my own. I noticed that one of the coaches was standing close by and keeping an ear open as Dortell was questioned. He almost seemed nervous, like Dortell was going to spill the beans about their strategy for the upcoming game, but he never interrupted him or spoke for his promising player. He just listened and watched.

I was busy taking my fake notes when something caught my peripheral vision. A fresh face had entered the locker room, and was slowly making its way through the throng and towards a player who was standing of by himself and disrobing. Something tugged at me and I turned to look at him.

The fresh face belonged to Jerry Pine.

EIGHT

It was him. I was sure of it. He was one of the Jerry Pines I had pulled up yesterday and listed as either Jerry 2, 3, or 4. Just the same, I pulled out my phone and navigated to the camera function. I turned off the auto flash and the audible shutter click sound, switched it to continuous shot mode, and then put it up to my ear like I had a call coming in.

I stepped away from the reporters and angled my body in such a way that the camera lens was facing toward the Jerry and the football player. Then I depressed the soft key, and held it down.

After a few moments, I figured I had gotten enough shots and said into the phone, "Let me see if I have that email."

I pulled the phone away from my ear and quickly went through the photos. I had gotten some good ones, and Jerry or whatever his name was, had on a press pass just like me. I selected one of the photos that showed the best view of it and zoomed in. The name on the pass read, Steve Pollard.

Nice, I thought; either this was an incredible coincidence and I had just happened to discover Jerry Pine's doppelganger, or he had a phony press pass just like me.

It made perfect sense though when I thought about it. Anyone who was supplying dope to the players would want to have easy access to them, and as I knew, impersonating a reporter got you about as close as possible without having to be on the staff.

I scrolled up to the top of the photo and to the nametag on the locker of the player Jerry Pine was talking to: Washington. Trevonte Washington was one of the other players that Tony had mentioned, and I thought that the dots just might be starting to connect.

I put the phone away and returned to the interview with Dortell, which was just wrapping up.

As the group of reporters broke away, I followed suit and moved off. I was keeping my one and only eye on Mr. Pine/Pollard.

He ended his conversation with the player and looked around the locker room at some of the other players. He looked suspicious, if not cagey. I didn't want to have him catch me looking at him, so I decided to leave the locker room and wait to pick up a tail on him from outside. At some point, he would have to leave the stadium area.

"Taking off, Jack?" Chris said from beside me.

"Yeah," I said absently. "I think I got what I need."

“Me too. Enough to pacify the editor ‘gods’ anyway,” he said mockingly.

Together we started walking down the hallway to the outside.

“I’d say let’s grab a drink and chew the fat,” the reporter said to me. “But I’ve got to get this in.”

“Me too,” I said, and just let it go.

Outside the perimeter fence that surrounded the stadium, I stopped walking.

“I’ve got to make some calls,” I said, pulling out my phone. “And the signal is shitty in there.”

“Got’cha,” Chris said and continued walking on. “Catch you later.”

As soon as he was out of sight, I turned my attention back to the stadium. Other reporters were starting to drift out, some still jotting notes and some already on their phones. I continued my vigil with the phone to my ear and was soon rewarded by the reappearance of my new target.

He walked right past me and didn’t give me a second look. When he was far enough ahead to tail, but not so far that I might lose him, I started walking.

He walked across the campus toward one of the parking lots. I stayed behind him, occasionally losing myself in a crowd of young students.

He entered the lot and made a straight line for his car down one of the rows. I moved two rows over, and stayed parallel to him and slightly behind. He pulled out his key ring, hit the fob and I saw the taillights blink on a silver gray Lexus.

I pulled out my phone, switched to camera and zoomed in on the license plate of his car. I snapped several pictures and knew I had all I needed to go on.

He pulled the car door open and was about to get it, when I decided that, just for fun, I was going to do one more thing.

I ducked behind an SUV, and looking through the tinted windows called out towards him.

"Jerry!"

He turned toward the sound and looked, but didn't see me.

Hellooooo Juice-Man!

NINE

After the outing of Mr. Jerry Pine, I left the campus of UCLB and headed back up the freeway and to home in Manhattan Beach. By now the traffic had been several hours into what is ironically termed “rush hour,” and it was stop and go all the way for the fifteen or so miles I had to cover.

I called Tiffany to apprise her of my situation, and when I finally got home around 6:30 we sat down to eat the leftover chicken pesto pasta as well as an arugula salad she had put together.

"I have my book club tonight," she reminded me as we were about halfway through the meal.

"Ah," I said. "I was hoping to relax on the sofa with you tonight."

She gave me a sidelong glance and said, "Oh Jack, you may be an expert liar and impersonator when it comes to your marks, but you can't fool me. You've got that look about you."

"What look?" I said, innocently enough.

"That look—like you just picked up the scent of something and are chomping at the bit to get on the hunt. I can tell that you must have found something out today, and you're anxious to get on with it."

Since I had come home, I hadn't mentioned anything to Tiffany about my meeting with Tony, or with locating the presumptive, Jerry the Juicer. This in itself wasn't unusual as I made a concerted effort to not bring my work home with me. Still, I must have I been advertising my barely contained eagerness and she picked up on it, and not for the first time. I don't think my own parents could read me as well as she could.

"Alright," I said, holding up my hands in surrender. "Yes, I discovered something today and yes, I'm anxious to follow up on it. But that doesn't mean I won't miss you."

She leaned over and kissed me then. "And I'll miss you," she said. "I'll be home by nine."

After we finished eating, I cleaned up the table and put all the dishes into the dishwasher while Tiffany ran upstairs to retouch her makeup and grab her things. She gave me a quick peck on the lips and then headed out the front door, a paperback with a colorful cover clutched in her hand.

"Have fun," I called out behind her.

Domestic chores completed, I climbed the stairs into my lair and got straight to work.

First off, I wasn't about to trust my judgement, and so I compared the photo I had taken with my phone to the ones I had found on the web of Mr. Jerry Pine. As it turns out, he was the one I christened Jerry Pine #4.

After a positive ID, I immediately began to dig further into every aspect of his life, starting as always with just the basics. He was fifty-three years old, twice divorced and lived rather modestly in a two bedroom condo in Lakewood, a bedroom community just north of Long Beach and UCLB. That was convenient, both for Jerry and for me, as I hated driving LA's freeways as much as anyone did.

He had no children from either of his erstwhile marriages and he paid no alimony or other support. He might have had property he had to split with his ex's during the divorces, but it looked like he came out with his shirt still intact on the other end. I next dug into his employment history, especially to see if he had once worked as a sports reporter, which could explain his phony press pass.

He hadn't and I thought, oh well, I knew as much as anyone that a phony press pass could be acquired easily enough. The Juice-Man had worked mostly in sales and, like many in the profession, had worked in a variety of disparate industries: casualty insurance, dental supplies, heavy machinery, fasteners, and then finally, athletic equipment.

Hmmm.

I looked further into the company he represented, Woorly Athletic, and found that they sold all forms of sports equipment for youth, high school, and most importantly, college teams. Every sport you could imagine was represented, from archery to wrestling, and Woorly, with its vast staff of expert reps, could satisfy all of your needs for everything from a Lacrosse stick to a shot-put, and to soccer balls in every color of the rainbow.

Double, hmmm.

I'd be willing to bet dollars to donuts that Jerry Pine's foray into the world of athletic equipment was just enough to wet his appetite into thinking that there were far bigger prizes to be had just over the horizon.

The Juice-Man was still listed as employed by the company, but was this just a facade to explain away some of his income? A lot of sales reps worked for numerous companies part time, as long as they weren't in competing industries. I checked his income tax records and found that he had only listed $49,417.39 as income from the prior tax year for his commissions from Woorly Athletic. Not enough to live on in pricey Los Angeles, and so I dug further into his return and then I found it, Jerry Pine's schedule "C" for business income and expenses.

My new friend happened to have a little side–biz going and one where he claimed the bulk of his income was coming from.

Gridiron Collectibles was a sports memorabilia company with Jerry listed as the sole proprietor. They had a website of the same name and the home page boasted that it focused exclusively on football memorabilia and collectibles. All of the memorabilia was broken down by category, and you could purchase vintage, as well as more current autographed photographs, football cards, and magazine covers. There was also an equipment side to the company, and it was here that you could get 'game used' jerseys, both framed and unframed, signed footballs from your favorite player, and helmets. In short, you could purchase just about any piece of football equipment you could imagine that might have touched a specific player's DNA—if only for a minute.

I looked at some of the prices listed for items and wondered how crazy people had to be to pay $899.00 for an Eli Manning autographed Newman High School green jersey? And then, I wondered suspiciously, if anybody would?

I went to Google and typed in the exact description of the item and hit 'search.' Several results came back and I navigated to the other sites, finding the same item listed for substantially less. I tried several other items listed on the Gridiron Collectables site and had the same results; everything they 'sold'—or at least listed—was overpriced. I began to smell a rat, albeit a crafty one.

I pushed back from the desk and stretched.

"I have to hand it to you Juice-Man," I said aloud. "You found a real nifty way to create a plausible income stream for your dope sales. You garner the bulk of your loot selling the PEDs, HGH, and steroids to the players, but you cover it all with phony sales of your memorabilia, of which hardly anyone purchases, because you have purposely priced it out of range. But, most importantly; you look clean to Uncle Sam."

I stepped away from my desk and took a quick break, brushing my teeth and using the bathroom. Already an hour had slipped by and it was eight o'clock. Tiffany would be home in another hour, and I debated if I should try to dig further into Jerry Pine's faux existence.

After a few moments of consideration, I decided that I probably had enough for now. I knew in my gut how the Juice-Man was getting away with it, but I still couldn't prove anything. Not just yet, and not with just with him setting up a Unicorn business. Connections needed to be made between the various parties in the dope pipeline. I had to continue by dredging up personal data on all of the players Tony had given me today, especially the top of the dubious athletic achievement pyramid himself, Mr. Dortell Williams. And so I dove back in.

For fans of TV detective shows, especially the reruns of the old ones from the seventies and eighties such as *The Rockford Files*, *Starsky and Hutch*, and *Mannix*, you would be disappointed to learn that the life of a PI—or of yours truly—was generally very dull. For the most part, I never woke up in the morning pondering how many car chases, shootouts, or encounters with beautiful women I would have that day. On second thought; I guess I *did* have an encounter with a beautiful woman every day.

Instead, the bulk of my day consisted of work that was painstaking, systematic, and worst of all, repetitious. And like a journalist who spends hours interviewing subjects, fact checking, and following up, in the end, I was lucky to use ten percent of what I found out, but that's just the way things cut.

The research into Dortell and his fellow suspect teammates—about seven of them in all—took up the next hour, and didn't garner much for me in the way of useful info.

Sure, I had all of their basic personal info: how old they were, where they lived, where they grew up, their familial situations, etc. I dug into their scholastic records as well as any employment history, but it wasn't much.

The dearth of information on them had as much to do with their youth as anything else. By twenty years old, most people had not yet established an arc of life with various jobs, marriages, places of residence, and so forth. Sure, a few had had some minor scrapes with the law, and one young man had fathered a child out of wedlock, but that was about it as far as anything that jumped off the page at me. For the most part, they had all lived at home, went to school, excelled at sports, and were awarded scholarships to UCLB for their talents. That was about it.

I leaned back in my chair trying to digest the information I had gleaned. It wasn't much and I knew it. The players were all pretty much the cookie cutter images of high school jocks that did well, and the routine drug testing program the school enforced had so far been unable to detect their pharmacological shenanigans. Jerry Pine had set up his little bogus sports memorabilia business to launder his proceeds from the dope sales, but I still didn't have anything that I could leverage to prove that he was indeed the Juice-Man, although I knew it in my gut.

I stood up and began to pace the floor, considering how best to proceed. First of all, I had to be able to prove that the players I was looking at were in fact, doping up. But how would I do that? The school tested them regularly as per NCAA guidelines, and either they knew how to cheat the test, or the testing hadn't caught up with the drugs that they were taking. I also knew that, based upon what I had read about PEDs, HGHs, and Steroids, that the drugs and the testing methods to detect them were a bit like the *Mad Magazine* cartoon, *Spy Vs. Spy*. First one side would win, and then the other. New drugs were developed, and then the testing methods had to change to detect them. Then the drugs changed again, and the cycle started anew like a game of Whack-A-Mole. It was a vicious circle with only the careless or the unlucky ones getting occasionally caught.

This left only two possible ways for me to snare either Jerry, the players, or all of them together in my little web. The first of these was to get them to admit to cheating, which seemed about as likely as being able to build an igloo on the surface of the sun. I had nothing on the players, and all I had on Jerry was a phony press pass and his phantom business. If I braced him about it he would most likely suggest I perform an anatomical impossibility, and just change his MO. At this point, he already had the relationships built up with the players and all I would accomplish is becoming a minor inconvenience in his otherwise proven business plan. That left catching one or several of them irrefutably in the act, and then leaning on them to rat out the remaining coconspirators.

I let out a big breath of air, contemplating such a course of action. Catching them with their pants down—no pun intended—would require extensive monitoring and surveillance, something that ate up oodles of time. I could tap the Juice-Man's cell phone, but to do that would mean I would have to get close enough to him to pair it to my device. Besides that, which phone would I tap? He might have several, or use disposable burners to conduct his dirty business on. He seemed like a smart cookie and had his tracks covered pretty well up until this point.

I heard a chime coming from my computer just then that signaled that our alarm system had detected that the front door had been unlocked and opened. I looked at the screen and saw that the CCTV system had switched on and it showed Tiffany stepping through the door.

I took it as my cue, and shut down the computer for the night before heading downstairs.

By the time I got down to the living room, Tiffany had already kicked off her shoes and was settling in on the couch with a glass of wine.

"May I join you," I said.

"I insist," she replied unequivocally.

I poured myself a glass and sat down next to her. On the coffee table was a book with the title, *Digging Too Deep.*

I laughed when I saw the title.

"What's so funny?" she asked.

I nodded toward the book.

"I feel like that's what I've been doing tonight," I said, laughing "Digging too deep. How was the meeting?"

"It was great," Tiffany said, "I'm really enjoying this group. Right now we're reading cozy mysteries."

"Oh," I said, taking a sip of my wine.

"Yes," she said excitedly, pointing to the book with the rim of her glass. "And this one is really good."

"What's it about?" I asked, happy to have someone else beside myself having to unravel a mystery, even if it was a fictional character.

"It's about this British woman—Cornish actually—and she's a gossip columnist for a newspaper, but she oversteps her bounds."

"How is that?"

"By digging up some dirt on the Royal family."

"A woman after my own heart," I said wryly.

Tiffany laughed.

"Oh yes," she said, emphatically "I'm sure you two would get along swimmingly."

"But she gets in trouble for trying to expose this scandal with the royal family in her newspaper column, and so she gets sent off."

"Sent off?" I repeated, feeling something beginning to churn in my brain, like pieces of a puzzle starting to drop into place.

"Yes,' Tiffany went on. "Her editor sends her off to the States until the bru-ha-ha blows over with The Royals. So she's exiled, I guess. Not in prison exactly, but kind of."

“Sent off,” I repeated again, hearing an eerie strangeness in my own voice.

I set my wineglass down on the table, and stared off into the distance, silent.

“Are you okay Jack?”

“Yes,” I said. “I’m fine. Great, in fact.”

Without knowing it, Tiffany had just given me the missing clue I needed to catch Jerry Pine and the rest of The Juice Gang.

TEN

I turned off the Antelope Valley Freeway in Lancaster, California, noting that I was now in a different world, a world far and away from my pampered life living the dream in one of California's best beach communities. This was the high desert area north of Los Angeles. Behind me was the San Gabriel Mountain Range, which separated the area from the rest of the LA proper. To the west was the Tehachapi Range, and far to the east, the San Bernardino Mountains. To the north, and just up the road from here, was Edwards Air Force Base, the place where Chuck Yeager first broke the sound barrier, as well as the dry lake bed where the space shuttle used to land.

The land out here would have been nothing but desolate and barren, had a housing boom not ensued in the early nineties that drove Angelenos away from their urban and suburban residences northward in search of more affordable digs. Since then, housing tracts, mini-malls, schools and roads all had multiplied like Jack Rabbits on fertility drugs, transforming this once sleepy desert town into one of the fastest growing burbs in America.

I turned west onto Avenue J, and before long, signs began to appear, directing me to my destination. The signs read *California State Prison, Lancaster, California.*

There were basically two types of people that I dealt with in my business: people who had a lot to lose, and people who had nothing to lose. The former category represented, for the most part, my many targets. These were the ones whose dirty little secrets—if exposed—would result in, at a bare minimum, embarrassment. But more often than not, the consequences could be the potential loss of a marriage, a job, or maybe even some jail time. They were the ones that required a stick to make them cooperate, a stick provided by yours truly in the form of a threat to lay their secrets bare to the world unless they played nice and followed my easy payment plan.

The other type of people to whom I would occasionally consort subsisted in the latter category: the ones with nothing to lose. They were the men or women whose lives had already been stripped to the core, who often had no money, no social standing, and no chance for a future. It was with this group that all I needed to do was to provide a carrot, a glimmer of hope, an opportunity to somehow improve their lot, if even a tiny bit, and they would do or say just about anything I needed. After all, it was said that a drowning man will grasp at a razor blade.

Kayvon Jackson was just that kind of guy.

A former premiere free safety for the UCLB Dolphins, he failed a drug test and lost his scholarship one year ago early in his junior year. With no education or work experience, his job prospects were dim, and he soon returned to the streets and to his former life of petty crime to survive. But he made a costly mistake when he upped his game from simple car and residential burglary, and followed others of similar leanings into an ill-fated bank robbery attempt.

Although Kayvon never pulled the trigger himself, an innocent man was killed in the botched attempt, and he was charged with among other things, accessory to second-degree murder. Since then, he had been cooling his heels in here for the past year or so, with another long twenty-four to go. His was a sorry existence, devoid of much hope. I was here today to offer him a smidgen.

The prison was a large facility at two-hundred-sixty acres and housed approximately thirty-five hundred inmates, many of whom were serving life sentences with no possibility of parole, a designation known as LWOP. A level 4, or maximum security facility, it retained the highest levels of fortification, both physical and human. Concertina wire enveloped the perimeter, along with a high voltage fence that could deter even the most desperate of escapees. Wary guards with automatic weapons were stationed in high towers every few hundred feet, and kept a watchful eye over the inmates' every move.

After waiting for approximately an hour in the visitor waiting area, I was finally asked to step forward and go through the security screening process, which was very similar to that of an airport. Before going through a metal detector, I emptied my pockets, took off my belt and watch and then removed my shoes, placing everything into a plastic tub. I was about to step through the detector when the correction officer (CO) performing the screenings stopped me.

"Hold it," he said. "I need to see you remove your eye patch."

I kept my expression neutral and complied with his order, pulling it off over my head and handing it to him. Then I stared at him in the face, letting him take in the grotesque peep show he had solicited.

Instantly, I got the reaction I was expecting. I saw his Adam's apple bob in his neck and his body recoil slightly. He swallowed and tried to keep his composure in front of me. He failed miserably.

You were the one who wanted to see it pal, I thought to myself. And now your lunch is ruined.

He quickly handed it back to me and amazingly, from that point on, I didn't have any more issues with security.

I walked the short hike over to the inmate meeting room and sat in there with a dozen or so other friends and family of the state's wayward residents waiting for Kayvon to be processed in. The room was about the size of a large classroom, and had tables and chairs set up here and there. The tables were purposely low to the ground in order to keep contraband—drugs, cell phones, or weapons—from being passed between the visitors and the inmates. Along one wall was a series of vending machines for snacks and drinks, and grim looking COs stood by watching every move that was made. Security cameras were everywhere.

About fifteen minutes after I arrived, Kayvon was led into the room by another CO. He was wearing the same two-tone blue scrubs that many of the other inmates had on, as well as special state issued brown leather prison shoes that were required for visits. The special shoes prevented outside visitors from surreptitiously switching identical looking shoes containing contraband under the table with the inmates.

I nodded to Kayvon and he moved over to the table I was seated at. He sat down without me offering him a seat, and I had a good look at him.

Based on the position he once held with the Dolphins, he was smaller than what most people would consider football player material. Although it was tough to estimate his weight under the loose fitting scrubs, I judged him to be only a hundred and eighty pounds max. He had a smallish head, and his hair was cut close to his scalp, maybe only a quarter inch in length. He had a pinched nose, smaller lips, and a set of dark eyes that stared intently at me. They were eyes that, on the surface, tried to tell me that he was in charge, but underneath, we both knew better. I didn't waste any time with chit-chat, and got right to the point, unbuttoning the sleeves on my long sleeve shirt.

"Fuck, it's stuffy in here," I said, loud enough so that the guards who were standing watch around the room could hear me.

After unbuttoning them, I rolled both of my shirtsleeves up, revealing my forearms, which were completely tatted up with a mosaic of designs. Buried within the designs were two portraits of men, one for each arm, and one of whom was Jerry Pine.

"Recognize either of these guys, Kayvon?" I asked quietly.

He glanced at them quickly and then back up to my face.

"Maybe," he said smugly.

I smiled back at him, a knowing smile. I was going home after this; he *was* home.

"Alright," I sighed. "Let me tell you how it's going to be, Kayvon. I know an awful lot about you. And one of the things I know is that you make about fifteen cents per hour working in the laundry in here. You work forty hours a week so you get, on average, a whopping twenty-six bucks a month. How am I doing so far?"

He didn't say anything, and took a big breath through his nose, causing his small nostrils to flare slightly.

"But that's not the whole story, is it?" I continued. "You've got restitution to pay back for your crime, don't you? So you have to give up sixty percent of your big paycheck every month, and that's about sixteen bucks. So you're really only netting about ten bucks a month, right? Shit, that's less than a kid in an Indian sweatshop makes."

Something was changing in his face; it was either anguish or anger, probably a good dose of each. I continued on, dispassionate of his expression.

"Now I also know that your family hasn't got any money to send you Kayvon, and I know that all of your friends have bailed out on you. So you're stuck with the whole bill for your restitution, all four thousand, eight hundred and ninety-one dollars of it. And do you know how *fucking* long, at sixteen bucks a month it will take you to pay it back? It'll take you twenty-five fucking years, Kayvon! That's your entire sentence! Do you really want to be scraping by for the next quarter of a century in this shithole with only ten bucks a month to spend? Or, would you rather be able to buy that extra blanket, or that magazine, or a can of Coke from the machine?"

He continued to stare at me, waiting for the penny to drop. I let him burn for a bit and then finally said, "So if you want to make the best of it in here for the rest of your stint, you play ball with me. You do that, and I'll erase *all* of your restitution."

That last statement did it. He broke. His eyes brightened like man dying of thirst spotting an oasis in the desert. His eyes shifted quickly over to my right arm. It was the arm with the image of Jerry Pine.

"Dude on the right," he said. "You right arm."

"Good," I said. "Now we're getting somewhere. So now you tell me about him, everything."

Kayvon glanced furtively from side to side. His voice dropped a few decibels.

"But dude says he's connected, man," he said softly.

"He's not," I said. "But I am: *The Ride*."

I saw the focus of Keyvon's eyes change to fear. He knew I was invoking the casual term for NLR, or the Nazi Low Riders, one of the most violent of all white supremacist gangs in prison. Nothing could be worse for an incarcerated African American than to be in their crosshairs, or, as they say in prison, "Have a green light on you."

"Alright," he said nervously. "I'll talk if you clean up my debt."

"I will; every last cent of it. So what's his name, first off? And how do you know him?"

Kayvon looked around conspiratorially, as if the place was filled with informants from the UCLB football team.

"Jerry," he said finally. "Jerry Pine. Dude sold us drugs. Not street shit, mind you, steroids, PEDS, that kinda stuff. You gots to take it if you want to stay in the game."

I nodded as if the blanket statement were as undeniable as the existence of gravity.

"So I've heard," I said. "Anything else?"

"Yeah," Kayvon dropped his small head and nodded. I noticed a tiny scar on the top of his noggin and wondered where he earned it, inside or out?

"The shit to clean it up," he continued. "You know; the drugs to prevent it from being detected."

I barely stifled the urge to laugh out loud, thinking wryly that it was akin to a rattlesnake biting you and then selling you the anti-venom. Kayvon missed it and went on. I could sense him easing up, which was good.

"But sometimes that wouldn't work for you. The testing would get better and then you'd have to get you some clean piss. Jerry sold us that as well."

I shook my head, realizing there was another whole crazy world out there that defied logic. Could our ancestors ever imagine people buying and selling urine?

"So how'd you get busted?" I asked. "If Jerry was your one-stop pharmacy and kept you fully supplied?"

"I dropped my Wizzinator," Kayvon said sadly.

"Your what?"

"A Wizzinator," Kayvon replied easily, as if every household had one. "It's this thing, looks like a dick. You fill it with clean piss, pull it outta you pants when they ask you to piss. You squeeze it in the middle and the piss comes out, all natural looking and everything. Even comes in different colors for whites, Hispanics, and blacks."

"And you dropped this, this…Wizzinator thing?"

"Yeah. Got popped for a random drug test. I filled it with clean guy piss and kept it warm with the heat pack that comes with it. But I guess I didn't have it attached right, 'cause when I unzipped my pants and pulled it out, I dropped it right in front of the dude who was watchin' me. I guess now they make you drop you pants all the way, not just you fly. Want to make sure you junk is connected to you."

"So you got popped with that," I said. "But how about the drugs that work to mask the PEDs? How do they work?"

"Work? Hell, I don't man. I ain't no fucking chemist or shit. They just do, for a while at least."

I switched gears, realizing that it wasn't that important at this point.

"So how'd you get all this stuff from Jerry? Where did you pick it up?"

"Off campus," Kayvon said adamantly. "Always. You'd see Jerry from time to time at practices and shit—he had a phony press pass so he could get in."

"I know," I said. "The name on it is Steve Pollard."

"You know that shit?"

"Yeah," I said, and moved on. "So where did you make the deals? How did you put in your orders?"

"Text him. Tell him you need some more stuff. He'd give you a price and a meeting place and time. It was all in code-speak shit, in case anyone checked your phone."

"Just like regular dope dealers work," I offered.

"Yeah," Kayvon said, and glanced at some of the other tables. I wondered wryly how many former dope dealers were sitting in this very room and having family visits right now.

"So how did you pay for this stuff when you were playing?" I asked. "I know that you didn't have a job while you were going to school, and I know that your family doesn't have any money. Where'd you come up with the scratch?"

Kayvon leaned back in his chair and seemed to relax a little more, like it was a fond time in his life to reminisce over.

"Easy," he said. "I sold tickets to the game."

"You got tickets?"

"Yeah, depending on how well you was playin', the coaches would hand out some good tickets to you. And then they'd tell you that so-and-so alumni wants to buy them. The alums would give you like a grand a ticket for something that had a face value of about sixty bucks."

"Whoo," I said. "Quite a mark-up. Good money if you can get it."

"Yeah and then they'd set up this other shit for you, little jobs where you'd make bank for just showing up half the time. Like working at a party the school supporters and alumni would have. You valet they cars for em, and they'd give you like a five-hundred dollar tip. That's how you made you money, man. That's how you survive as a student athlete."

"And the coaches were all in on it, right?"

"Shit yeah man!" he cried incredulously. "They the mother fuckers that set all the shit up. They's all making big bucks on their shoe deals and shit. Everybody getting bank. They just wanted you to keep playin', and not have to take a real job that would interfere with practices and shit."

"Makes sense," I said, "But do you think they did it knowing you would use the money to buy the dope?"

"Probably," Kayvon shrugged nonchalantly. "Everyone wants to win, man."

I let the last statement hang in the air. Winning, whether it was wars, politics, or sport, man had an unquenchable thirst for victory.

But I didn't have any time to ponder the foibles of my fellow homo sapiens, and moved on in my inquiry. Now that I understood—the how and the when and where of the UCLB doping universe, I need to know the *who*.

"So who else is doping at UCLB, Kayvon?" I said. "I need names, current players."

He looked at me for a long time, considering.

"They kill me man if I dimed em," he said finally. "I can't."

"They aren't going to know it's you," I said. "I swear."

He took a breath and scratched at the side of his head, still considering. I prodded him along.

"It's either trying to pay off your restitution and rotting in this dump with no privileges for the next quarter of a century, or you go along with me. You do that, and I erase it all with one Paypal transfer into your trust account. They don't need to know who snitched em out, and they won't. I promise."

He stared at me and I could see that drowning man reaching for that razor blade again. He took in a deep inhale of air.

"Alright," he said, and began to list off names, telling me what they were taking and for how long. I recognized a lot of the names as ones that Tony had given me as suspect players, but one was conspicuously absent.

"What about Dortell Williams?" I said.

"Demon?"

"Is that what you call him?"

"Yeah, that's his nickname."

"How'd he get that name?" I asked.

Kayvon stared straight at me and I noticed that there was something in his eyes, fear maybe.

"Because he runs like a man possessed," he said.

ELEVEN

"A man possessed?" I repeated.

"Yeah. I seen him after some fricking amazing runs and shit. He's all wild eyed and crazy looking."

"This is at practice?"

"Nah. Never in practice—we only run three-quarter speed then—just in games. Sometimes coach would have me go both ways, and I'd play split end or slot, mostly as a diversion or possibly for bootlegs.

Then the ball would get handed off to Dortell and that mother-fucker take out two linebackers and pass me like I was standing still."

"So then he's juicing, right?'

Kayvon shook his head.

"I don't know man. I never heard him talk about it, never seen any shit go down."

"Maybe he's just real careful, Kayvon." I offered. "Did you ever think of that?"

"Could be," Kayvon said and let it hang in the air, like a mystery that would be forever unsolved.

I felt that I had all the information I could glean here, and started to stand up to leave. Kayvon followed suit. I unrolled the sleeves on my shirt back over my forearms, and buttoned them over my wrists. Kayvon nodded to my forearms.

"By the way, pretty clever puttin' the dude's mug on you arm. You think like an inmate."

I nodded. Before I came up here, I checked the rules for visitors, including which items could be brought in or not. At one time, the policy allowed visitors to bring in up to ten pictures, as long as they weren't Polaroids, and as long as they all were brought back out. But about three months ago, the rules abruptly changed. It was discovered that a hit had been ordered on an inmate from the outside when a picture identifying him was brought in by a visitor.

I could have tried smuggling the pictures in, but I didn't want to risk it. So, I turned to one of LA's best tattoo artist and had him 'sleeve' me up—including the images of Jerry and my decoy—in temporary henna ink. In a couple of weeks, the tattoos would be nothing but a memory.

Kayvon changed gears then and asked me when the money would go into his account.

"As soon as I'm in my car and turn on my phone, I'll send it right over via Paypal. I'm sure it will take a couple of days to process, but you'll be clear of your debt before you know it."

"Thanks," he said, and we shook hands.

I easily made it back through the security checkpoint, returned to my car and as promised, logged onto my Paypal account and transferred four thousand, eight hundred and ninety-one dollars into Kayvon's account.

The transfer complete, I pulled up my left shirtsleeve and pressed the buttons on my G-Shock watch. To the casual observer, it looked like a regular, no nonsense, and inexpensive watch. But it was developed by the FBI as discrete way to 'wire' informants. It had a tiny MP3 recorder built into it and I had switched in on as soon as I cleared security. Without knowing it, Kayvon had just given me the audio confession I needed to nail his former teammates.

Just like the coaches, the players, and all of mankind, I really liked to win too.

TWELVE

"Wow! I still can't believe we're here Jack," Tiffany said.

I threw my hand up to my chest as if I suddenly had heart palpitations.

"What?" I mocked incredulously. "You don't consider me a proper squire, a gentleman who would not treat his lady to sights and sounds she may not have been privy to prior to our Affaire de Coeur?"

We were seated four rows up and midfield at the UCLB football stadium. It was just moments away from kickoff in what was touted to be the game of the season between the hometown Dolphins and their arch-rivals from up north, the Stanford Cardinals. Both teams were 2 – 0, and this game could set the momentum for the rest of the season.

"No. It's not that," Tiffany said, having to raise her voice above the growing din of the crowd. "I just knew that you never cared about sports."

"I never have," I admitted. "But now I've got a vested interest."

By now, I had assembled a lot of what I needed to move forward and set my little plan into action: I had Jerry the juicer, I had knowledge of how the system operated, and I had a list of players that I could soon begin to lean on. But one nagging piece of information had eluded me to this point. Who was the "Demon," Dortell Williams? And if he wasn't juicing, how the heck did he pull off superhuman feats of strength and speed?

Over the past couple of days, I had studied the stats and highlight reels of his past performances, and they were almost impossible to believe with your eyes. I knew then that I had to see it for myself.

"And for your information," Tiffany continued. "I *have* been to a college football game before, *Squire Jack*."

"Maybe so," I countered. "But have you ever sat on the fifty yard line?"

Another roar went up in the crowd around us just then. The Dolphins had just won the toss and elected to receive. On the sidelines, coaches and assistants barked out orders and the special teams units took to the field. Dortell Williams doubled as a return specialist and went out with them, taking a position back at the Dolphin's fifteen-yard line.

The Dolphin faithful began to chant, *"Demon...Demon...Demon!"*

"Maybe, maybe not," she yelled. "How did you get these tickets by the way? I read that this game has been sold out for months."

Incredulous, I turned and looked at her, arching my eyebrow. Had she forgotten what her boyfriend did for a living?

Tiffany started laughing at my antics, and then wrapped her hands around my biceps and pulled herself closer to me. It felt nice.

"Never mind," she laughed, "I'm sure there's a great story behind it."

And there was. His name was Patrick Hannigan, and he was one of the top ticket scalpers in LA. Besides the sundry sporting events and concerts most of his ilk procured, he also could get tickets for just about any event you could imagine: Academy Awards, Playboy Mansion parties, film premieres—you name it.

But he crossed the line when he decided to make a couple of easy bucks by selling tickets at inflated prices for an upcoming visit by the Pope to Los Angeles. Having been raised in a devout Irish-Catholic family, the very thought of making illicit profits on an appearance by the pontiff would be nothing short of heresy with the rest of the Hannigan clan.

When I presented this egregious debasement of his faith to Patrick and reminded him that his parents still had a sizable estate to which he would be cut out of if they ever gained knowledge of this fall from grace, he did what any good Catholic would do. He confessed his sin, made an act of contrition, and asked for forgiveness as well as his penance for absolution. I figured that besides a nice monthly stipend, I should also be entitled to top cabin tickets to any event I wanted. For a guy like Patrick, it was an easier pill to swallow than endless Our Fathers and Hail Marys.

Even from our seats this close to the action on the field, we could barely hear the bleat of the referee's whistle signaling the start of the game. The Stanford kicker raised his arm into the air, then marched forward and booted the ball high and deep into the Dolphin's territory.

The ball hung in the air for several seconds, allowing Dortell to adjust himself under it, before catching it with both hands. Then he took off like a bullet fired from a gun.

The stadium erupted into wild cheers as he broke tackles one after another with incredible speed and agility. It was like the other players were standing still.

At about the forty-yard line of Stanford, a few defenders that had hung back zeroed in on the Dolphin speedster. Dortell surprised everyone when he didn't run toward the sidelines to avoid them, and instead turned directly toward his attackers. He hit them in a violent collision that sent the two men flying backward like bowling pins.

He stumbled a bit from the collision, but was able to regain his footing. In a futile, last ditch attempt to stop him from scoring, the Cardinal's kicker ran towards the UCLB superstar, but it wasn't even a contest.

Dortell crossed the goal line and dropped the ball into the end zone as the roar of the crowd filled the stadium. A few seconds later, a few of the Dolphin blockers caught up with him and they exchanged celebratory chest bumps and helmet hits. Even though he had just run the equivalent of a world class 100-yard dash, Demon was still jumping around and seemed bursting with energy. I thought back to what Kayvon had said about, "a man possessed." What the hell was this kid taking, and who the hell was he getting it from? It was starting to drive me crazy.

"Wow!" Tiffany yelled. "I've never seen anyone run like that before!"

"Me neither," I said, and I watched as Dortell and his teammates moved off the field. The players around him were trotting to the sidelines, but he still seemed like he wanted to run, and was overflowing with vigor.

The extra point was good, and it was now seven to zip Dolphins with less than a minute played. It could turn out to be a long afternoon for the Stanford Cardinals if things kept going this way.

While the teams were changing squads from offense to defense, I took a few moments to look for familiar Dolphin players in the mix. I had memorized the jersey numbers of most of them that were juicing, and wanted to study their play while I was here. But I also took the opportunity to check out the stadium in general.

It had been a long time since I had been to a sports venue, and things had changed quite a bit; everything had gone modern and high-tech. There were several Jumbotron displays set onto the top of the stadium walls and the enormous monitors were showing playbacks of Dortell's amazing run, as well as close-ups of the Dolphin cheer squad doing their routines.

There were also the occasional random shots of faces in the crowd. More times than not, these 'random' shots were the die-hard fans that had painted their faces in the school colors of teal and gray, or wore silly hats that looked like the head and snout of a bottlenose dolphin. When the fans noticed their images displayed onto the Jumbotron, they would immediately stab their finger up into the air and could be seen mouthing the words, *"We're number one! We're number one!"*

Besides the giant monitors, a banner of LED lights encircled the field just above ground level. The lights were in lieu of hard billboards or banners, and changed constantly, beaming out advertisements for everything from car insurance to fast food to credit cards. Every once in a while, an advertisement for UCLB would be seen, as well as the occasionally and obligatory touting of the piety of the NCAA.

I glanced to the Dolphin sideline, and noted that the coaches and assistants had gone high-tech as well. Gone were the clipboards of old with sheets of plays and formations on them. Instead, most of the staff now had tablets in their hands that they were continually swiping and moving icons around on. Smartphones, tablets, and other devices, the world was wallowing like pigs in a digital orgy.

The offensive coordinator I had seen standing by Dortell in the locker room the other day was talking to him and showing him something on his tablet. My guess was that it was either a review of his phenomenal run, or a series of upcoming plays the coordinator wanted him to execute.

Dortell seemed to have mellowed by now and was off his post-run high. In a very short time though, the Demon Dolphin would be right back at it and burning up the field.

* * *

If there was a weakness with the Dolphin's team, it seemed to be on the defense side of the ball. On their first offensive series, the Cardinals answered the UCLB touchdown in a six plays and put up eight points of their own by scoring a TD and converting.

But the Dolphins weren't going to go rest on their laurels and hang the outcome of the game strictly on the shoulders of their star offense. They continually and adroitly adjusted the defense, and before long they were holding the perennial favorite Cardinals to plenty of three and outs. And just about every time they would retake possession of the ball, the Dolphins would continue to score, typically on the back of incredible runs made by Dortell.

The final score was 52 to 14, in favor of the Dolphins which put their record at 3 – 0. I knew that the airwaves and social media would be going wild with speculation as to how far they could go.

Like many of the other spectators, Tiffany and I didn't wait to see the denouement play out and started to head out of the stadium and to our car.

"What did you think, Jack?" she asked me as we were leaving.

"Good," I said. "Very entertaining."

"So do you think you'll get 'hooked'?" she teased. "Am I going to become a 'football widow' now?"

"Not hardly," I said, and we both laughed.

I held her hand and we continued on to the parking lot in silence. I was going back over the game in my mind, but mostly the fantastic runs by Dortell.

Under pressure from my father, I had played football in high school, but only for a season and a half. I wasn't very good, never started, and didn't enjoy being a human tackling dummy for the better players.

Still, I could try to imagine what it must be like to make the amazing plays that Dortell and some of the others were executing—even if it was done with aid of drugs. The roar of the crowd, the adulation of your fans and teammates, and the pure rush of adrenaline from moving so fast and deftly had to be intoxicating.

And addicting.

THIRTEEN

Ted Kowalski entered The Platter Restaurant in Long Beach with more swagger than I thought was humanly possible. After angling his huge body sideways to come through the doorway, the UCLB lineman began to scan the interior to find me.

I lifted my arm and waved at him. He grinned a self-assured grin and strode past the other booths and diners toward me like he owned the joint. He was dressed in a pair of blue nylon running shorts that came down almost to his knees, and a teal and gray Dolphin T-shirt which was straining to the point of bursting with his giant chest, thick neck, and biceps the size of bowling balls.

Although, Kayvon had given up plenty of names of players that were dirty, Kowalski seemed like the obvious choice to lean on. Along with Dortell Williams, he was considered a top contender to enter the draft, and would probably have a long list of pro teams vying for him and ready to offer him a fat contract. That lofty financial upside catapulted him into the category of someone who potentially had a lot to lose if they didn't play along with me, and those were my favorite kind of people to do business with. Besides that, the bigger there were, the harder they fell.

After a bit of shoe-horning, he wedged his massive body onto the seat across from me. As soon as he sat down, I felt the whole booth shake as if a Sherman tank had just rolled by us. He extended a thick arm across the table to shake, his giant mitt reminding me of a Grizzly bear paw. His hand completely enveloped mine and I hoped he wasn't the kind of guy who had to prove his manhood to you by crushing your hand in his. Thankfully he wasn't, and I was able to retract my appendage intact and no worse for wear.

"So Sports Illustrated wants to interview me, huh?" he said without preamble. "Yeah, I was wondering what was taking you guys so long."

Just as I had figured, besides his massive torso and limbs, Kowalski also had an outsized ego. It was a minor miracle that his swelled head had fit through the door to the restaurant along with everything else. With that amount of braggadocio, I wouldn't think that it could squeeze through the Panama Canal.

I smiled and said, "Yes," almost feeling like the big lug was expecting me to get down on my knees and beg for forgiveness for the magazine's tardiness.

A waitress was at our table a moment later and set a couple of menus in front of us. Kowalski looked around before picking his up.

"Never been to this place before," he said, matter of factly.

I nodded and smiled.

"I thought it might give us a little more privacy," I said.

Rather than meet him in one of the coffee shops or fast food joints near the campus that were popular with the student body, I purposely picked this place for the meeting today. It was away from the school, and catered to an older crowd of diners and families, which made it decidedly "un-hip." And this déclassé standing made it less likely that we would run into any of Kowalski's cronies or adoring fans. It also had large booths with high walls separating us from the other diners which would offer a degree of privacy should things get dicey. I would be dropping a bombshell today, and I didn't need big number sixty-seven to cause a scene.

After scanning our menus, the waitress came back and took our orders: a BLT and coffee for me, and four double cheeseburgers, three orders of fries, and a pitcher of Coke for Kowalski.

After he ordered his feast, he stared across the table at me, grinning like Cheshire Cat and looking like he was waiting for a reaction, like "Wow!" or

"Oh My God!" But I wasn't going to give him that; his ego was already big enough for ten men. Besides that, I was about to ruin his appetite anyway.

"So where do you want to start?" he asked smugly. "I'm sure you guys want to know who I want to play for."

"Actually, this is where I want to start, Mr. Kowalski," I said, and pulled out my wallet. I flipped it open to reveal a perfect replica of a Drug Enforcement Agency badge.

"Jack Roberts, United States Drug Enforcement Agency," I said very officially.

Kowalski's jaw dropped slightly and he leaned forward to examine my badge. I noticed that his face had lost a bit of color.

After a few seconds, I flipped my wallet closed and put it back into my jacket.

He pushed back into his seat, and I felt the booth shudder again.

"Wha-what th-the fuck?" he stammered, his eyes narrowing. "What do you want to talk to me for? I don't do dope; I'm an athlete."

“We understand that Mr. Kowalski,” I said calmly. “But we’re not talking about cocaine or heroin here; we’re talking about steroid use and illegal performance enhancing drugs.”

He shook his massive head vigorously. How it could swivel without benefit of a neck, I couldn’t comprehend.

“I don’t juice, man,” he said emphatically, and a little too quickly. “I’m clean. Get my piss checked all the time. You can check the records; you got the wrong guy.”

“No we don’t,” I said. “You’ve been identified along with several of your teammates.”

I pulled out my phone and hit play. The recording was a distorted copy of Kayvon’s admission to me at the prison the other day. Altered or not, Kowalski’s name was clearly recognizable in the playback, along with the names of the drugs he was taking.

When the recording was done, I switched it off, put the phone back into my pocket, and waited. Just like a jilted lover or someone who had just lost a loved one unexpectedly, learning that your dark secret had been discovered triggered a broad range of emotions. In order, they typically went something like this: disbelief, denial, anger, admission, and then finally, surrender.

The big lineman skipped the first couple of reactions, and headed straight for the one I was expecting him to.

"Fuck that man!" he bellowed. "Whoever said that shit is a fucking liar!

Just to accentuate the point, he stabbed his finger at me angrily. It was about the size of a Kielbasa.

"And I'll kill them with my bare fucking hands if I ever find out who it is!"

"No you won't Kowalski," I said flatly. "And keep your voice down and your 'roid rage in check; there are civilized people in here. You're already in big trouble, and seeking revenge is only going to add to your woes."

"Oh yeah! Says who?" he demanded to know.

"Says the United States Drug Enforcement Agency," I said. "Which, I shall remind you, is under the US Department of Justice. And the DOJ doesn't take kindly to murder threats, especially towards individuals who are cooperating with an investigation. You go off trying to wring someone's neck, and we'll hang you from your little steroid-atrophied balls. You got that?"

The waitress returned and brought our food just then, the available real estate on the table shrinking significantly with the delivery of Kowalski's personal banquet. Hopefully, the food would have the same calming effect as music did on the savage beast.

We were both quiet and civil during the food's delivery, which pleased me. When she turned and walked away, Kowalski just sat there and glared at me silently, not touching his spread. Go ahead I thought, let your food get cold, you big palooka. I stared back at him, smiled and then picked up my BLT and took a bite. He tried to unnerve me by continuing to stare, but it wasn't working.

Finally the aroma of the food got to him and he picked up one of his double cheeseburgers. He chomped into it, and roughly one-third of it disappeared in a single bite. Without setting his sandwich down, he grabbed the pitcher of Coke by the handle, tilted it sideways and drank straight from it. A class act this guy.

"So, what do you want from me?" he asked right before taking another massive bite.

"Cooperation with this investigation," I said, taking a sip of my coffee. "You help us nail the guy selling you the drugs, and we'll go easy on you."

"I told you," he said emphatically. "I'm not doing or buying any drugs." He reached over and picked up the ketchup bottle, unloading about half of its contents onto his fries. He grabbed a handful and shoved them into his mouth, ketchup running down his chin.

I took another bite of my BLT, and wiped my mouth off with my napkin. I'm sure my table manners were as foreign to him as they would be to a tribe of cannibals.

"Yes you are Mr. Kowalski," I said. "And the man you're getting them from is named Jerry Pine, although he has a press badge that says his name is Steve Pollard. He supplies you, and everyone else on that recording, with steroids and the PEDS, as well as the drugs to cheat the tests. And we need your cooperation to help get an indictment on him."

"Hmmm," he mumbled, acting like he was mulling it over when in reality, I knew he was already starting to get scared and was stalling for time. He wiped his mouth with the back of his hand and then fisted the pitcher again and took another long drink. By now, only half of the contents remained. Kowalski wasn't exactly a cheap date.

"And what if I don't feel like cooperating with your investigation," he said defiantly, smirking at me as if he was holding a straight flush in his hand.

I smiled right back. "Then you'll probably need this," I said, and handed a sheet of paper to him.

He shoved what was left of his burger into his mouth, grabbed the paper in his big paw and scanned it.

"What the hell is this?" he said, before he had finished chewing his food.

"It's a job application for this restaurant," I said easily. "I took the liberty of getting you one in case you needed it. They're hiring dishwashers and busboys."

"Screw that!" he said indignantly, tossing the application down on the table, it landed on top of his fries and began soaking up the ketchup. "I don't need that shit!"

I leaned forward and lowered my voice a few decibels. It was time for him to realize just how tiny a corner he was painted into.

"You will need it if you decide not to cooperate with us Mr. Kowalski," I said softly. "We go to the NCAA with this tape, and you'll be immediately dropped from the team. You'll also never get into the NFL draft based upon their new zero-tolerance policy. So that leaves your college education, which is only half complete. And which, based upon the conditions of your scholarship, you will forfeit the remainder of when you are no longer able to play ball for UCLB. After all, you signed a contract with them. And the quid pro quo was four years of free education, for four years of playing ball."

I paused for a bit to let it permeate his thick skull and then added, "And just how many career opportunities do you think are out there for a half educated, sociology major who was convicted of illegal drug use, Kowalski?"

I glanced toward the job application lying on his ketchup soaked fries; a dark stain was already spreading on it.

"So either you pick that up and fill it out, or you play ball with us and have a chance at the big leagues. It's up to you."

He rubbed his chin with his big hand, his eyes darting about desperately. He looked like he had lost his appetite.

"But he…Jerry, he's connected," Kowalski said, and I realized how sick I was of hearing that.

"No he's not," I said. "He's already been checked out by our organized crime unit at DOJ. He just says that to you so you guys will be afraid of him."

The last statement did it, and Kowalski sprung up in the seat across from me just then. It almost looked like he had snapped to attention. I should have known that it would trigger an almost Pavlovian response in him. Inside, I kicked myself for not realizing how to play this dolt sooner.

"I'm not afraid of him!" he said emphatically. "I'm not afraid of anyone."

"We know that, Mr. Kowalski," I said, nodding. "And that's why we selected you for this assignment. You're the only man we could trust to complete the mission."

"You're damn right!" he beamed.

FOURTEEN

Now that he was part of 'The Mission,' the big lineman idled down a few thousand RPM, and reached for his second burger. Between his monstrous appetite and his enthusiasm for being tabbed for the assignment, I wondered wryly if I had asked him at that moment to swallow some microfilm if he would have done it.

"So what do I gotta do?" he said as he was busy inhaling his burger. "Wear a wire?"

"Not exactly," I said. "Let me see your cell phone."

He stopped in mid chew, suddenly suspicious.

"Why?" he asked.

"Because that's how we do things these days," I said. "Since everyone carries a phone, it's just as easy to use it as the transmitting device as having someone wired up. Does Mr. Pine ever search you, or ask you to surrender your phone when you get the drugs from him?"

"No."

"Does he ever tell you to remove the battery from your phone?"

"No."

"Good," I said. "Then hand me your phone."

My explanation didn't do much to mollify him, and Kowalski studied me as if I was trying to sell him the Brooklyn Bridge. I didn't budge and stared straight back at him. Finally, he acquiesced, pulled out his phone and set it on the table. I took out my own phone, tapped a couple of keys and set it next to his.

"What are you doing?"

"I'm pairing your phone to mine and installing an app," I said. "It clones your SIM card, and will allow the DEA to listen to your conversations, watch your emails and texts as a third party. It's called blue hacking."

He started to reach for his phone, and I reached out to nudge his hand back; it was like pushing a holiday ham.

"I don't know if I like this, man," he said. "I talk to a lot of people and girls and stuff. That's an invasion of my privacy."

"We don't really care if you don't like it or not, Mr. Kowalski. You have agreed to cooperate with our investigation and this is the way it's going to be."

My phone chimed, telling me that the pairing was complete. I picked it up and put it back into my pocket. He slowly reached for his own phone and picked it up. He turned it over cautiously in his hand like it was radioactive.

“Now that we have that done,” I said. “Here’s what you are going to do. You’re going to contact Mr. Pine and order some more drugs, the same kind and quantity that you currently take.”

“But he’ll be suspicious,” Kowalski said. “Because I just got some last week and started to cycle.”

I thought about it for a moment.

“Tell him you fucked up,” I said. “Tell him you were clumsy and dropped them into the toilet, and that you need some more of the same and the drugs to mask the test.”

The big lug listened and considered my work-around. He seemed convinced that it was a plausible story, and so I kept going.

“You contact him on this phone and this phone only,” I said emphatically. “And you keep your phone with you, and turned on during the buy. You don’t have to do anything more than that. You won’t see us, but we’ll be listening, and you’ll be watched.”

I reached into my pocket, retrieved an envelope from my pocket, and handed it across the table to him.

“Here’s the buy money,” I said. “Three grand, just like you told me. It’s already marked. Don’t spend any of it, and don’t even mix it with your other money. This is important so we can nail him.”

The reality set in just then about what he was about to do and Kowalski looked suddenly filled with dread. His face drained of blood.

He was silent and thinking. The waitress came by and replaced the nearly empty pitcher of Coke with a full one. When she moved away, Kowalski picked up the pitcher and drank about a third of it. Then he looked at me.

“I’m kinda worried,” he said. “I never done anything like this before. What if I get nervous and fuck it up?”

“Don’t worry, Mr. Kowalski,” I said emphatically. “We know that you won’t fail us. The government of the United States of America has the utmost confidence in you.”

That brightened him right up and he grinned.

“Yeah, you’re right” he said.

His big mitt reached for his third double cheeseburger. He picked it up and took a bite.

Half of it disappeared before my very eyes.

FIFTEEN

The buy between Kowalski and Jerry Pine was to take place at *The Grinder*, a local coffee shop popular with the UCLB students. It was located just a few blocks away from the campus, and served the usual fare of pastries, heat and serve sandwiches, yogurts, smoothies as well as a dizzying array of coffee drinks.

It was a Friday and the day before the game, so Kowalski had an abbreviated practice session today. I was fortunate that tomorrow's game was against the USC Trojans, just a short drive up the freeway from Long Beach at the Los Angeles Memorial Coliseum. Otherwise the big lineman would have been travelling with the team today and I would have had to wait another week to set up the buy.

I didn't go into the coffee shop lest I was spotted by Jerry Pine, and instead sat outside in my car watching. Just the same, I wasn't about to take any chances that Kowalski wouldn't get me the damning evidence I needed, and so I had a man already stationed on the inside who would record video and audio of the whole thing going down.

His name was John Fallon. He was a struggling actor that I used from time to time for such low-level work as this, and he welcomed the nice paydays it provided while waiting for the calls from Steven Spielberg that never arrived. He had been sitting at a corner table inside The Grinder for about a half-hour now, nursing an iced coffee and ostensibly working on his laptop. The laptop was one of mine and had been specially modified for such work. The top cover had an HD camera discreetly installed in it and facing outward. From his display, Fallon could watch what was being recorded and pan it, or zoom in or out.

It was about 1:35 when I saw Kowalski pull into the parking lot in his car. The buy was set for 1:45 and so far I hadn't seen any sign of Jerry the Juice-Man. Even though I had set everything up as carefully as I could, there was always a chance the dealer would get suspicious and blow it off, or at the last minute come up with a new location. But there was nothing I could do about it at this point except sit and wait, and to reassure my stooge that everything was going to be okay. I dialed Kowalski's cell phone and he pulled it out and answered it just as he was slamming the door to his car. He started to head toward The Grinder.

"Hello."

"It's Agent Roberts, Mr. Kowalski." I said very officially. "You are doing just fine. Just go inside and do like you always do when you are making a purchase."

"Okay," he said, and I thought I detected a tremor in his voice. I could hear him swallow audibly through the phone.

"I just thought of something," he said. "If I'm going to have my phone on during the buy, what happens if I get a call or a text? Is that going to screw the whole thing up with the recording? Am I going to have to go through this shit all over again?"

Internally, I had to give Kowalski a modicum of credit for thinking ahead about all the things that could go wrong during an operation. Most criminals never think of any of the crazy possibilities that could derail a perfectly deep laid plan: a person screaming, traffic snarls, a door opening suddenly—that's why criminals get caught. Credit to my lackey or not, it was just a modicum he would earn today, as I had already planned for that prospect.

Besides monitoring his calls, texts, emails and location at all times, the app I installed on his phone also gave me the ability to block selected voice or data traffic in or out from the device. From this point on, the only calls or texts that could go into or out of Kowalski's phone were with me, or Jerry Pine.

"We've already taken care of that," I said as Kowalski was reaching for the front door. "Only calls or texts from me or Mr. Pine can go in or out of your phone during the buy."

"You mean you're blocking my calls?" he cried indignantly. "That's BS man! I got this chick calling me about a party tonight. I don't like this man."

"Well it's too late for that Mr. Kowalski," I said firmly. "Unless you'd like to call the whole thing off and we go to the NCAA with the evidence we have on you. Is that what you want?"

"No," I heard him say softly, and then I heard a muffled conversation as he gave his order to the barista: Three ham and cheese sandwiches, two Danish, and a Trenta Cold Brew, a concoction which contained so much caffeine, the container it came in could have been classified as hazardous waste.

He pulled the phone closer to his mouth and continued, "I just don't like an invasion of my privacy man."

“Well that’s just a damn shame Kowalski,” I shot back. “Maybe you should have paid better attention when you were little and heard the expression, *cheaters never prosper*. Just do your job.”

“Fuck you man!” he said. “I gotta get my food and grab a seat. They’re going fast.”

“Alright,” I said. “Just remember to keep your phone on the table face up at all times so we get good audio.”

“I will,” he said, and then hung up on me.

I pulled the phone way from my face and scrolled through the icons until I got to the surveillance app. I activated the microphone in Kowalski’s phone, and immediately started to hear the bustle from inside the coffee shop. Orders were being called out, pots clanked, and a phone rang in the background. People were laughing.

“In a few moments I heard Kowalski’s voice say, “Thanks,” followed by the clank of coins dropped into the tip jar. I wondered if it was him, or someone else; he didn’t strike me as the kind of guy who felt he owed anybody anything.

A few moments later I heard the scrape of a chair as it was dragged across the floor. I started to record the audio.

I had gone back and forth with myself on whether or not to tell the big lineman that his calls would be blocked during the buy. As always, there were pros and cons to how much information you wished to divulge, but in the end I decided that, based upon his personality and frenetic protection of his privacy, if I told him, I would get the response that I needed.

It's an old trick practiced by drug smugglers, con artists, and other sundry scumbags, but unknown to the average law abiding citizen; the best way to get through a stressful situation when you have to be deceptive, is to not be in a 'normal' disposition. You need to act tired, or annoyed, or ill, or in Kowalski's case, angry. Any one of these—or a combination of them—does well to overwhelm and mask any underlying fears or anxiety you might have. Now that Kowalski was pissed off about his phone being compromised, it would be easier for him to not tip his hand to the Juice-Man.

Speaking of the Juice-Man, he pulled into the parking lot of The Grinder just as my phone chimed that a text had come in from Johnny Fallon. The message read, “The big boy just sat down. Good angle on him and whoever else is going to join him.”

I replied to the text with a single “Thumbs Up” emoticon, and then turned my attention back to my target.

Jerry Pine got out of his car, locked it with the key fob, and strode across the lot and into the shop without bothering to look around. Perfect; he looked nonchalant and like this was just another routine delivery for him.

He stepped into the shop and a few seconds later I heard him say, “Hi” to Kowalski.

Kowalski said, “Hi” back, and I didn’t detect any fear in his voice. “How’s it going?”

“Fine,” Jerry Pine said. “You got the money right?”

“Yeah. You got the stuff?”

“Yeah.”

“Good,” Kowalski said. “I just started to cycle again, and didn’t want to break it.”

"Then don't drop your stuff into the shitter," Jerry said unsympathetically. Real focus on customer relations, this guy.

"Yeah, Right," Kowalski agreed. "Here's the money."

I heard some shuffling, some sort of an exchange, but I couldn't tell how the transfer was being made. It didn't matter, as I would see it all on Fallon's video later anyway.

"Okay," Jerry Pine said. "We're good. Call me if you need anything else."

I heard the scrape of a chair, and then Kowalski's voice again.

"Will do," he said.

And that was it.

Jerry Pine exited the coffee shop and headed back to his car. In a few moments he was headed out of the lot and on to who knows where next. The whole thing took less than two minutes.

I got out of my car, went into The Grinder, and sat down in the chair at Kowalski's table that Jerry Pine had just vacated. It wasn't even warm.

I noted that in the short amount of time that Kowalski had been here, he had already polished off two of his ham sandwiches, and one of the Danishes. The Trenta cup was half-empty. I wondered if I should have contacted the Guinness Book of World Records right then and told them that I had just discovered the world's largest tapeworm.

"Very good Mr. Kowalski," I said. "Now let me have the merchandise."

He slid a small envelope across the table toward me and I put my hand over it before palming it, and dropping it into my pocket. Kowalski picked up his Danish and made half of it disappear like he was starving. I cut him some slack as he probably hadn't eaten for maybe what…thirty seconds?

"So I'm off the hook right?" he asked.

"You cooperated and did well. You won't be charged and we can keep it quiet from here on out."

I started to get up and leave. As I was pushing my chair back in Kowalski stopped me.

"So what happens to the drugs?" He asked, gesturing to my pocket.

"They'll be analyzed by a team of top scientists at the DEA," I said easily. "They'll figure out how to work around the mask, and detect the drugs."

"So then that means that…"

"Yes," I said. "These drugs are now useless, to you and to everyone else. They're a poison pill, and anyone who takes them will be detected and booted out by the NCAA."

"Shit!" he said angrily. "That sucks. I need them if I want to stay in the game."

I shrugged and stared down at him. Kowalski sat there, his big blockhead hanging down, his expression as forlorn as a child whose balloon had just been popped.

What the idiot didn't realize was that this was a gift. He now knew that these particular drugs would soon become detectable, but other athletes didn't. That increased his odds for getting into the NFL as more college athletes would test positive and be out of the running for the draft. I could have explained it to him, but I decided to let him stew; he wore anger well.

"My advice Mr. Kowalski…" I said, and he looked up at me.

"Get clean," I said, and walked out of The Grinder.

*   *   *

I was nearly to my car when I heard someone call out.

"Jack!"

I turned toward the sound and saw that it was Chris Moore, the reporter from the Los Angeles Chronicle that I met the other day at the UCLB locker room. He was walking toward me. I stood there and waited until he caught up to me at my car.

Moore looked as dapper as ever, and was dressed in a pair of charcoal gray pleated slacks, a steel blue long sleeved shirt, and a bow tie in black and gray stripes. The bow tie was done in a diamond point shape, and didn't appear to be a clip-on or pre tied. I was impressed and I'd bet he folded hospital corners on his bedsheets.

He didn't extend his hand to shake as I would have expected and instead said, "I was surprised that you turned around when I called your name."

"What do you mean?" I asked, puzzled.

"Well I just figured that the name Jack Roberts was as phony as everything else about you," Chris Moore said.

SIXTEEN

We stood there looking at each other for a long time, our eyes locked. But instead of his usual easy smile, the reporter regarded me with a hint of disdain, as if he had been taken advantage of.

Inside, I was disappointed in myself as well. I should have realized that journalists are a naturally curious bunch, and that many harbor desires to be the next Bernstein or Woodward of *All the Presidents Men* fame. Even the laziest of hack reporters would have done a cursory search of Chicago tribune looking for the bylines of Jack Roberts. I was lazy and sloppy when I blurted out my breezy fabrication of being a former reporter with the paper.

I thought of my options, which were few and shaky at best. I could just turn and walk away, which would probably only work to stoke his inquisitiveness further. And it could very well make me persona non grata in the locker room if he decided to spill the beans on me.

I could have said that I wrote under a pen name, but I doubt that he would have bought it and then possibly ask me to produce some of my work. So I decided to make lemonade out of the lemons life had tossed my way. If Chris Moore was in fact such a dogged sleuthhound, then maybe I could leverage this current predicament in my favor.

I let out a big sigh, swiveled my head and surveyed the parking lot nervously. Then I turned back toward Moore.

"You got a few minutes?" I said.

“Sure,” Moore said, not changing his expression.

I gestured back toward The Grinder and we walked toward it in silence.

Before we reached the entrance, Kowalski, having decimated the remainder of his meal, exited the coffee shop and started heading toward his car. Seeing me with the reporter from The LA Chronicle rattled the big lummox even further. I had already overloaded his pea brain with my yarn about an undercover DEA investigation, and this just threw gasoline on the fire. Tough for him.

The crowd was beginning to thin out, so we found an empty table in the corner of the shop right off the bar. His assignment for me complete, John Fallon was also in the process of shutting down his laptop and getting ready to leave. When he saw me walk in with Chris Moore, he didn’t react and kept his expression neutral; he was after all, an actor.

I took the outside chair, leaving the inside corner one to Moore. He looked a little bit suspicious, but I didn’t care. It would all be clear to him soon. Before he sat down, I noted that he brushed the seat of the chair off, lest he pick up any crumbs on his slacks.

When we were both seated, I reached into my jacket and removed my wallet. I opened it to my badge and held it up for Moore to see, but no one else.

"Special Agent Jack Roberts," I said flatly. "DEA."

If there was a silver lining in this dark cloud spawned by Moore's surprise appearance, it was that in having to meet with Kowalski today, I wisely chose to bring along my fake DEA badge on the off chance that the lug wanted to examine it again. Having it with me now would help me immeasurably when I had to lay it on thick to the young reporter.

Moore studied the badge, looking for any telltale signs that it was a fake. He wouldn't find any. I had a great forger I was leaning on who kept me stocked in perfect replicas of just about any form of ID I needed. And sometimes, having the highest quality documents meant the difference between getting away with impersonating an individual or not.

I hope that this encounter would be of the former variety.

"We're working on an undercover investigation," I said, closing my wallet and replacing it in my jacket. "An investigation into wide spread doping of college athletes."

"At UCLB?" Moore asked.

I nodded and then added. "And at other schools as well."

Moore used the palms of his hands to flatten out his perfectly pressed slacks and regarded me for a long moment, considering. His reticence in buying the story on just a badge and a statement was actually something I admired, and if it swung my way, something I could also use. He was a fact digger and a fact checker. Good qualities to have if you're a PI or a journalist or if you are going to unwittingly help out a character like me. Still, just producing a badge and story wouldn't be enough; I had to come up with a plausible scenario that would fill in any holes that popped up.

"Really," he said, skeptically. "I thought you guys just had a big bust with Operation Cyber Juice in two thousand and fifteen. That didn't clean the house enough?"

I had to give Moore lots of credit, as he really knew his stuff. Cyber Juice was a sweeping operation comprised of over thirty different U.S. investigations in twenty states that resulted in the arrest of over ninety individuals and the seizure of close to a metric ton of steroid powder and millions of dollars in currency. For many agencies it would be just the sort of plum that would cause them to rest on their laurels for a bit.

"Under normal circumstances, yes," I admitted. "As big and successful as that operation was, any other time we'd all be patting ourselves on the back and plotting out our next career moves. But with all of the attention being paid to CTE now, and a possible link between it and doping, we've been given marching orders not to be taking a victory lap and to get our butts back to work."

I paused dramatically for a second and then added, "This comes all the way from the top, Mr. Moore."

The last statement got the reporter's attention. His eyes grew a little bit wider, and I could see his see his pupils dilate. At the same time, his phone went off that he had a call coming in. He pulled it out of a holster on his belt, looked down at it, and then slid the soft button to ignore. He looked back up at me. His demeanor had changed.

"You're kidding?" he said.

"No."

"The president?"

"That's right," I said emphatically. "We all know that he's a huge fan of the game, and he doesn't want to see anything besmirch America's favorite sport."

"Whew," Moore whistled out. His boyish face broke into a grin like he had just discovered the Lost Dutchman Mine. He anxiously reached into his shirt pocket and pulled out a notepad and a black and platinum Mont Blanc pen. I held up my hand.

"No, Mr. Moore," I said. "This is an active investigation by the DEA and the Department of Justice, and we can't have you compromise it by taking any notes or recording any of this. And you have to promise me your complete and unwavering cooperation and confidentiality."

He didn't return the notepad and pen to his pocket and instead set them on the table. The man probably had a mind like a steel trap and didn't need them anyway. Still, he looked disappointed.

"So I'm not going to get a story?" he said sadly.

"Not yet," I said. "Not until the investigation is complete, and certainly not if you blow the lid off of this for us."

"You mean like you practically blew the lid off of it with your bogus Chicago Tribune reporter story?" he shot back. "That was pretty dumb."

I took in and then blew out a big breath of air.

"I told my supervisor that it was thin," I grumbled. "And that I needed a better cover story. Asshole thinks he knows everything."

Not that I felt I needed to—as everyone who's ever worked has had to tolerate incompetence from a superior—but just to put an exclamation point on it, I stabbed my finger toward the young reporter angrily.

"And that bastard's never once been in the trenches like me!" I snarled. "But he wouldn't listen."

"Sounds a lot like journalism," Moore said wryly.

"I'll take your word for it," I said, ratcheting down my ire a few notches. Then I returned to the topic of the need for him to keep this under wraps.

"And speaking of words," I continued. "Can I trust you to keep this to yourself until we conclude the investigation?"

"And I get a story then?"

"Yes, you have my word. As soon as I'm cleared to do so."

"An exclusive?"

I raised my hand up to my face and rubbed at my goatee like I was considering how much to promise.

"We're not supposed to," I said, and saw Moore deflate a little bit.

Then I smirked and said, "But there's always a way, Mr. Moore.

I leaned toward him across the table conspiratorially and said, "Let's put it this way; the other reporters are going to be in your vapor trails picking up crumbs and trying to piece a story together, while you just might be on your way to Columbia University."

I had him then; I knew it. Just the mention of the esteemed university where the Pulitzer prizes are doled out every year would be enough to secure his taciturnity. After all, why would he want to spoil his chances at the big time by sharing this kill with the other lions?

"You got it," he said happily, then added. "So how's it going with the investigation so far? Can you tell me that?"

"We're doing okay," I said, noncommittally. "We've got some names; we know how the juice is getting to the players and so forth. But one thing has us baffled."

"What's that?"

"Not what, but who," I said. "Dortell Williams."

"He's not a part of this investigation too is he?" Moore asked.

"Yes. Why wouldn't he be?" I said. "He's fast, way too fast to not be juicing. But we can't seem to get any evidence that he's taking anything."

I paused and then added, "Could you shed any light on this, Mr. Moore?"

The young reporter leaned back in his chair and weighed the question. His full lips squeezed together and he reached up to his face and rubbed his chin. It was smooth as a baby's behind and I wondered if he could even grow facial hair.

"I don't think he is," he said after few moments. "I hear lots of things and I've never heard any rumblings that he's on the juice. Plus, he's got none of the telltale signs of usage."

"That's true," I agreed, and then I pressed further with something else that was nagging at me.

"So what's the story with the Dolphin Offensive Coordinator?" I asked.

"Ken McCormick?"

"Is that his name?"

"Yes. What do you mean, what's the story with him?"

"He seems really protective of Dortell, practically hovers over him. I watched him the other day in the locker room."

Moore laughed and his lips curled upward into a patronizing grin.

"Did you ever play sports Mr. Roberts, in high school or in college?" he asked.

"Not really," I said. "A little in high school. I was never anything."

"Exactly!" Moore stabbed the air with his finger like he was putting an exclamation point in the air between us. "You just don't get the sports thing, Mr. Roberts. Dortell is McCormick's blue chip. And coaches get real protective with their premiere players—almost to the point of paranoia. They watch them like a hawk to make sure they don't get into any trouble. You know; get mixed up with the wrong crowd, injure themselves snowboarding and stuff. Hell, if they could wrap them up in a padded suit, put them away on a shelf, and only take them out on game day, they would."

I shook my head and leaned back in my chair. "I guess you're right," I admitted. "I never understood the ‘mystique’ of great athletes and why they are put up on a pedestal.”

“If you keep hanging around in locker rooms you will,” Moore quipped.

“Maybe so,” I said. “But even forgetting McCormick’s smothering, if Dortell isn’t juicing, how do you explain his performance on the field?”

“Easy,” the reporter smiled, “The Demon’s just one fast mother-fucker.”

SEVENTEEN

Chris Moore and I spoke for just a few minutes more before we said our goodbyes and went our respective ways. I had his number in my phone and I gave him a special burner number to call me on if anything came up.

I arrived back at our home in Manhattan Beach and after parking and securing the car in the garage, stepped inside the spacious three-story structure. Tiffany's car was still in the garage, but that didn't mean that she was home. She could have gone out for a walk, a bike ride, or got picked up by one of her girlfriends and gone out shopping or whatever. I didn't think that was likely though; as she didn't leave any note for me on the kitchen counter, or call or text me to tell me she had gone out.

Rather than check every room or start calling out to her, I pulled out my phone and skewed through the live video stream from our security system. I located her in a few minutes, up on the top deck and sunbathing. She was topless.

The drive home from Long Beach and my dual meetings with both Kowalski and Moore had put me in a fog. With Kayvon Jackson's statement from the prison the other day, the statement by Kowalski, the dope in my pocket, and the video of Jerry Pine doing the deal, I easily had enough dirt to go after any one or all of them. And if only ten percent of the players made it to the NFL, I could easily set up a nice new revenue stream for myself that would pay out for several years. Yet, for some reason, I couldn't care less about it, and I really needed to talk to Tiffany about it. I felt like I was losing it.

I chose the stairs over the elevator and climbed out onto the top deck where she was sprawled out half-naked on a chaise lounge. She turned toward me when I opened the door. A pair of Versace sunglasses in red frames covered her eyes.

"Hey baby," she said, when she saw me.

"Hey," I said back.

I stepped over to her and leaned over to kiss her. Her lips were warm from the sun.

She was wearing white bikini bottoms with spaghetti straps and a tiny front panel the size of a playing card that barely covered her pubic region. The swimsuit top was on the table next to her, along with her phone, suntan lotion and a fashion magazine. Even in the fall, she was managing to keep her tan and avoid any lines. Her skin was smooth, bronze, and delicious.

I slid another chaise lounge next to her and sat down on the edge.

"Not worried about paparazzi flying over and getting shots of you for some supermarket tabloid?" I asked.

"Nah," she said easily. "It's when they don't care about you that you have to worry." She then added, "But a little drone did fly over and hover for a while."

"Oh? Did you take it out with the surface to air missiles I gave you?"

She shook her head.

"Nope. I just set my top back on and waited the pervert out," she laughed. "He got tired and moved on to better eye candy."

"No such thing," I said hungrily, and she took my hand and laid it on her bare breast. I began to gently knead her nipple between my fingers. Soft moans soon escaped her sumptuous lips, and her hips began to squirm and gyrate.

After a few seconds, she pulled my hand away.

"Alright," she said, breathless. "Enough. We'll pick this up later."

"Absolutely."

"So, how was your meeting?" she asked, changing the subject.

I looked away and out through the sheets of clear Lexan toward the Pacific Ocean.

"I don't know," I said distantly.

"What do you mean, Jack?" she asked, concerned.

"I just don't understand myself," I said, turning back to her. "I've got everything I need to set this whole thing up now. I've got the dope supplier, the names of the kids juicing, all the evidence to back it up, even the pills themselves, and yet I don't even feel like moving forward. It's like I've lost my motivation. I'm so distracted by this one kid, this Dortell Williams. Hell, I'm not distracted; I'm obsessed with him."

Tiffany sat up in her lounge chair.

"He was that speed demon we saw the other day at the game, right?"

"Yeah, and I feel like I'm losing it because all I can think of is trying to figure out if he's juicing, and if so, how? Even though everyone I've talked to say's he's not. Plus, I get a weird feeling about the

Offensive Coordinator—his name is Ken McCormick—and his relationship with Dortell."

"Why's that? Tiffany asked.

"He practically hovers over Dortell, and it makes me suspicious. Moore—this reporter guy I talked to today—says that it's completely normal and that coaches are like that with their promising players."

"Makes sense," Tiffany offered.

"Yeah, but I can't seem to convince myself that he's not hiding something. Maybe he's feeding him some special juice and doesn't want anything or anyone to pollute the water so to speak, so he keeps him on a short leash."

I shook my head like I had voices inside driving me batty.

"Logically, I know that I should just ignore the two of them and move on to do the smart thing business wise."

I looked over at her.

"But I don't want to. I want to keep digging. Am I losing it, Tiffany?"

“Jack…Jack…Jack…” she chided. “You’re not losing it. This is just who you are.”

“What do you mean?”

“I mean that this is *you,* Jack. The same Jack I’ve known for a couple of years now. The Jack who has to turn over every stone, understand everyone’s MO. You’re like a maniacal treasure hunter, searching to the ends of the earth until you find every last gem, every last piece of nugget of gold. And you won’t quit until you do.”

“So you don’t think I’m crazy for being fixated on this one kid, and the offensive coach, even though it makes no sense?”

“Oh, I still think you’re crazy, Jack,” she laughed. “And yes, it’s totally illogical for you to push the sure thing to the side and focus on the one bird in the bush instead of all of the ones in your hand. But like I said; that’s just you. And I know that you’ll go crazy if you don’t find out what’s going on with them.”

Then she added, “And you’ll drive *me* crazy in the process.”

"I thought I already drove you crazy," I winked.

"Oh you do," she smiled seductively. "In the best of ways. But I know I'm going to have to wait until after midnight for you to prove it."

"What do you mean?" I asked, although I knew what she was getting at.

She pulled down her sunglasses and looked me directly in the eye.

"You know what I mean Jack," she said smiling. "You've got to find that hidden treasure."

"Yeah, I know," I said, smiling back at her.

I leaned over and kissed her deeply, then stood up and headed back inside to my office.

It was going to be a long night.

EIGHTEEN

Back in my office, I log back onto the Emperium website and I began my data mining where I always did, with just the basics. A California native, Kenneth Charles McCormick currently lived in Belmont Shores, a trendy, upscale neighborhood in the City of Long Beach, only a short distance from the UCLB campus. He was married with no children to the same woman Cynthia Louise McCormick (nee Campbell) for twelve years. Mrs. McCormick worked as a registered nurse at Saint Joseph's Children's Hospital in the city of Orange and had so for the past four years. The couple had a combined annual income of over five-hundred thousand dollars, a good credit score and were putting money away into their respective retirement accounts. There were no outstanding liens or judgements against them, and they appeared to be a solid upper middle class couple.

I next moved on to Ken McCormick's career. Not surprisingly, he had been a standout player in both high school and college, and he made it to the NFL as a tight end after being drafted in the twelfth round. He played for three seasons in Los Angeles and then one season in Seattle before being released. After getting married, he headed north and played Canadian ball for a couple more seasons before returning to the US to take a position as offensive assistant in Dallas.

Life was good and the team's management must have liked what they saw, because within a few years McCormick moved up the ranks into the position of Offensive Coordinator. Then, in 2009, while the team was enjoying a 6-1 winning record and had the number three offense in the country, he unexpectedly left in the middle of the season. "And why is that Mr. McCormick?" I said out loud.

It didn't take much digging to find the cause of his sudden departure as the media had a field day with the scandal that was at its impetus. A young woman by the name of Pamela Jean Franklin, who worked with the team as an assistant equipment manager, had claimed that McCormick had sexually harassed her. The 'he said/she said' turned ugly as it played out in the court of public opinion for several weeks and apparently as a result of the charge, but without admitting fault, McCormick was asked to resign to keep the reputation of the team intact.

An admission of guilt or not, the damage must have already been done. The McCormick marriage suffered, and within a week of being asked to resign, his wife and he separated. They apparently worked to patch things up though, as I found some medical records for several months of counseling sessions. Their efforts must have paid off, as they reunited after seven months and as far as I could tell had been together ever since.

Just for general purposes, I bookmarked the woman's name in case I needed to come back to it and then moved on.

Released from his job with the pros, McCormick returned to the gridiron—albeit in a diminished capacity—as a head coach for several high school teams back in California, before finally being able to wrangle his job at UCLB. His stint with the Dolphins began the same year that Dortell accepted his scholarship and began to play there. Since then, the two have helped the team rack up impressive yardage and apparently, have become inseparable.

I sat back in my chair and laced my hands behind my head, staring at the screen.

It was an interesting story, but not all that unusual. McCormick was on the fast track, made a big mistake and paid dearly for it. It was a sordid tale that had replayed itself out infinite times and had derailed the careers of many a promising politician, CEO, or rising celebrity. Still, it didn't do one thing to answer the nagging question of why McCormick was so protective of Dortell. Did he see Dortell as his possible ticket back into the pros?

I went back into the history I dug up on Dortell to see if anything jumped out at me to tie things together. Nothing did. He was an okay prep player who eventually and dramatically rocketed into the limelight. And now he was the monkey on my back that I couldn't shake loose.

Before logging off, I checked the start time for tomorrow's Dolphins versus Trojans home game. Kickoff was at 1:15 PM. Good, I would be able to sleep in and take Tiffany to breakfast before we each had to go our separate ways. She had a new bass player she was working with and they had to get their riffs together.

* * *

When I finally called it a day and climbed into bed, it was just six minutes before midnight. Tiffany was asleep but she stirred when I slid in under the covers. She turned toward me and we started to kiss.

"I made it to bed before midnight," I informed her between smooches.

"Mmmm," she murmured. "Congratulations Cinderella, you won't get turned into a pumpkin."

"It was actually the coach that was going to turn back into a pumpkin," I corrected her. "But I get your point."

She moved tighter against me and I felt her pelvis start to work against mine.

"Get everything you needed tonight?" she asked me.

"Not everything," I said, hearing my own breath starting to come in impassioned gasps.

"Well then let me help you," she said and rolled over to her back. She pulled me on top of her and spread her legs.

I found my way between them and we made passionate love until we fell asleep in each other's arms.

Like she said, I drove her crazy.

NINETEEN

There is hype, and then there is college football hype, which has no peer.

After parking my car in one of the numerous overpriced lots across the street from the Los Angeles Memorial Coliseum, I made my way towards the entrance to the historic venue.

Built in 1923 as a memorial to the veterans of World War I, the City of Angels icon has hosted two

Olympics, several professional football teams, and was the site of the very first NFL-AFL championship game, aka Super Bowl I.

The feeling was as electric as any Super Bowl game as I walked along the grass of Exposition Park toward the entrance, dissecting a veritable human sea of boisterous tailgaters. Music blared from speakers, and the air was thick with aromatic smoke from barbecues cooking everything from ribs, to brisket, to plain old hot dogs. Some fans, impatient to see authentic action on the gridiron, had coddled together ad-hoc touch football games on the scarce patches of open grass.

I paid no attention to them as I navigated my way through the reverie. I wasn't here to party, to compare stats, or to dislocate my shoulder; I was here to witness everything I could about the bizarre ligature between McCormick and Williams.

By the time I made it through security and took my seat, the teams were already warming up on field, the stands around me beginning to swell with bodies. With their decisive win last week against the Stanford Cardinals, UCLB's record now stood at

3 – 0, making today's contest a pivotal game. Cautiously optimistic fans kept their fingers crossed amidst a growing buzz about a first national championship for the Dolphins.

Dortell Williams was on field in the third row, stretching with one leg bent at the knee and crossed over the other, and I quickly spotted McCormick lingering on the sidelines. He was splitting his time talking with other coaches, examining his tablet, and talking on his headset.

At 1:10 PM the game finally got underway. USC had won the toss and elected to receive, so I would have to wait until the ball got turned over to watch Dortell spring into action. More than keeping my eyes glued on the Demon though, I decided to split my attention today on McCormick and his actions. The last time I saw the UCLB Dolphins play, I was strictly focused on watching Dortell. Now I wanted to observe McCormick's behavior as well.

USC drew first blood by making a TD and the extra point in seven plays with the Trojan fans cheered wildly as the pigskin split the uprights. Sitting astride his trademark armored horse; Tommy

Trojan took a victory lap around the stadium to rally the faithful and taunt the vanquished, his broadsword cutting wide arcs in the air.

Unimpressed, the Dolphins headed out onto the field next to receive the kickoff with Dortell lining up deep in his own territory.

Not surprisingly, the kickoff was strategically angled and landed in the hands of another receiving back, DeSean Washington, a sophomore speedster who had transferred from Nebraska. He was good and fast, but not like Dortell.

He quickly moved the ball up the field about fifteen yards with Dortell angling in to block for him. The USC defense drew a quick bead on the ex-Cornhusker and started to hone in. When the closest Trojan was only five yards away and contact seemed imminent, Dortell suddenly dropped back and Washington deftly lateraled the ball to him. As soon as the Dolphin Demon had it in his hands, he took off like a rocket, angling himself to the opposite side of the field.

During all of the action, I stole a glance at McCormick to watch his reaction. Quite curiously, he alternated between watching Dortell streak across the field, and looking down at his tablet.

The Trojans caught a lucky break when Dortell got jammed up behind some of his own blockers and a USC defender nailed him from his weak side, putting the ball on the Dolphin forty-seven yard line.

I looked back at McCormick and saw him swiping his finger across the screen of his tablet and talking on his headset. The Demon hadn't even climbed to his feet yet and already the offensive coordinator was plotting his next move.

On the opening play of their offensive drive, the Dolphins took USC by surprise when they went to the air and completed the pass for an eighteen-yard gain and a first down in Trojan territory.

Now that they knew the pass game would work, UCLB went back to the ground offensive with Dortell moving to the slot back and taking the ball on a reverse. After the exchange was made, he streaked like a bullet through the weak side gap and along the far sideline and the Dolphin bench before the free safety was able to herd him out of bounds at the eleven yard line of the Trojans.

The Demon stayed upright the whole time, and with an endless well of intensity that was tough to fathom, he fist bumped and shoulder slammed his teammates on the sidelines as he hustled back out onto the field. The kid was like a hunk of uranium in a jersey whose energy output had a half-life of ten thousand years—with no sign of decay.

A screen pass on the next play failed to move the ball more than a couple of yards and it was second and goal for the Dolphins. They went with a no-huddle and set up in a split back formation with Dortell playing fullback on the strong side under the tight end.

I decided that after the next play series was complete, I was going to leave the stadium and return through another entrance with my bogus press pass. Now that I had gotten enough of bird's eye view of the action, I wanted to get closer to Dortell and McCormick.

The Dolphins lined up in a shotgun formation with Dortell at the halfback position showing block.

The quarterback lifted his leg, sending the weak side wide-out into motion. The ball was snapped and the QB dropped into a passing stance. The Trojan defense bought the draw like a Brooklyn Bridge deal and spread out to protect the end zone from the pass they thought was coming. In the meantime, Dortell took the handoff and was off to the races, charging straight up through the A-gap where a hole had been opened for him.

He made it through the crease and was almost into the end zone when the Trojan middle linebacker nailed him hard with a low hit. Dortell's body spun in the air in a 360° rotation and he came down on hard his left side. His body had none the less crossed the plane of the goal line, and the line judge raised both arms into the air signaling a touchdown.

The stadium erupted into a roar and Dortell sprung back up to his feet like nothing had ever happened. He jumped about wildly with his fellow teammates celebrating, and seemed even more animated than usual—if that was at all even humanly possible.

The special teams unit started trotting out to the field for the point after as Dortell and several others began heading to the sidelines. I stood up from my seat and was trying to squeeze my way out of the row to get down to the sidelines with my bogus press pass when I heard a collective gasp come up from the crowd. I turned and looked back down to the field.

Dortell had collapsed.

TWENTY

In a flash, a small swarm of medical personnel, as well as McCormick, raced out to the field. Dortell's body lay there motionless as they began the process of checking vitals and other indicators. A gurney was brought out as well as an oxygen tank.

By now, most in the stadium had stood up as well and were watching in stunned silence. I maneuvered back to my seat for the time being and remained standing with them.

After a few, agonizing moments, we all saw Dortell's leg straighten out and move under its own power and the crowd was able to breathe again. The staff and medical crew now had his helmet off and they were feeding him the oxygen. From up in the stands, it appeared that he was awake and talking to them.

McCormick looked pale and kept alternating between looking at his tablet and at his injured player.

In a few minutes, Dortell was put into a cardboard neck brace, lifted onto the gurney in an abundance of caution and was carefully transported into the locker room. The crowd remained standing and gave him a rousing cheer.

I took the opportunity to move out of my seat to make my way to the nearest exit. As I was walking past the snack bars and souvenir stands, I took out my phone and launched the UCLB live streaming radio app that I had downloaded. I wanted to track as close to real time what the sportscasters were saying about Dortell, as well as to get down to the field and snoop around as well.

By the time I reentered the stadium and made it down to the field and had stationed myself with the rest of the press corps near the end zone, the game had resumed and the first quarter was about to end.

The Dolphins had substituted another back for Dortell and had adjusted their offense accordingly. It seemed to have been paying dividends as the score was still tied up at seven apiece with the Dolphins having possession on the Trojans twenty-five. McCormick was on the sidelines and watching the plays go down. He still looked extremely worried and appeared distracted.

I pulled out a notepad and did a sham of taking copious notes about the game, all the while listening to the radio play in my ear. Between plays, the announcers would discuss Dortell's collapse and speculate as to whether or not he had sustained a concussion from being upended. They must have had a replay running in front of them, because they were insistent that he had not landed on his head. They did confirm however that the team doctors were taking no chances and were giving him a full exam, including x-rays.

The first quarter ended with the Dolphins in the red zone and within striking distance of another touchdown. Both sides took the obligatory time out before switching ends of the field and the players headed to the sidelines for instruction. The break gave the announcers a chance to analyze the first quarter to this point as well as give any updates on Dortell's condition, as they became available.

After retaking the field, the Dolphins went up again by another six points when the Trojan defense had a miscommunication that allowed a quarterback-keeper for UCLB.

The point after was good and the kickoff team took to the field when the announcement came over my earbuds that Dortell was okay, and that the diagnosis was that he might have been slightly dehydrated. Still, with coaches and trainers from Pop Warner all the way up to the pros on edge over concussions, it was decided that he would sit out the rest of the game as a precautionary measure. He walked back out onto the field under his own power, flanked by the medical personnel on each side of him and received another cheer from the crowd. He had removed his shoulder pads, but still had his pants and jersey on.

He fist-bumped numerous players on the sidelines and received hugs from several of them. Then he made his way over to McCormick. They exchanged a few words, and McCormick slapped him on the back. The offensive coordinator looked immensely relieved.

The game ended two hours later with the UCLB Dolphins besting the USC Trojans twenty-four to seventeen.

As the clock ran down to zero and the whistle finally blew, the expanse of green was suddenly transformed and looked like an infestation of cockroaches as players, coaches and a swarm of media covered it. There were the standard congratulations being offered between players and coaches as well as statements to the press. Lots of the USC players offered well wishes to Dortell as he moved about the field with his teammates.

Several of the coaches, as well as some of the players, were being interviewed by the media and I saw McCormick being peppered with questions from a couple of reporters. From my vantage point, the offensive coordinator looked distracted and kept staring off down the field. I followed his gaze and it led, not surprisingly, to his young charge, Dortell Williams. But it was what Dortell was doing that surprised me.

Along with about a half-dozen other players from each side on the far end of the field, he was down on one knee and praying.

TWENTY-ONE

The Guiding Star Church was one of many islands of hope that dotted the blighted urban landscape of South Los Angeles. It served those of the Baptist Faith and, like many, was a struggling enterprise. In spite of its hardships, both visible and hidden, it was popular with the devoted and had regular services as well as an active choir, youth ministries, a Sunday school, and a missionary unit that did occasional work overseas. The first Sunday services were at 10 a.m. and I pulled into the lot at about 9:30 to get the lay of the land.

The church was set off from the street at the back corner of a large, battle-scarred parking lot that had not seen a fresh coat of asphalt since gas cost fifteen cents a gallon. The church structure itself didn't look to be ready to fall down in a stiff breeze—at least yet—and was of straight gable construction with a Spanish tile roof and off-white stucco walls. Over the double door main entrance was a bell tower with an eight-sided portico. A frayed rope dangled from the ceiling inside the portico, but there was no visible bell.

Incongruent to the Spanish architecture were four ogival arch Gothic style clerestory windows in textured amber cathedral glass. One of the windows must have caught a stray bullet from a drive-by shooting because a strip of sun bleached duct tape ran diagonally across it. Rusted wrought iron security bars covered the windows from top to bottom. The bars covering one window were splayed apart from the efforts of an overly zealous—yet obviously unsuccessful—intruder.

Having been born out of wedlock to a woman who struggled with substance abuse issues, Dortell lived with and had been raised by his grandparents, Henry and Leona Williams since he was six years old. When he was eleven, his mother died of acute carbon monoxide asphyxiation, when homeless and desperate, she broke into an auto repair garage during the winter and decided to run a car to stay warm.

In spite of the tenuous circumstances he had been born into, Dortell appeared to have been raised in a stable household by a caring, God-loving and God-fearing family. He had never been in trouble with the law, made good grades in school, and lived about a half mile away from the Guiding Star Church in a modest, but tasteful two bedroom home.

Before long, the weekly pilgrimage had begun with vigor as cars began to pull in and the tired parking lot beginning to fill. Those exiting their vehicles were attired in their Sunday best, with the men all outfitted in suits, and the women in tasteful dresses, many with matching gloves and hats. Most beat a quick path straight to the front of the church where they congregated on the steps and fussed about, kissing, shaking hands, and laughing.

I had the make and model of Henry and Leona's car, as well as their plate number, and I kept my eye open waiting for them to pull in. But they surprised me, when at about quarter to ten, all three of the Williams' clan strode up the sidewalk and onto the church property. There were still plenty of parking spaces available, so I could only conclude that they had walked the short distance from their house over to the service. Nice, and environmentally friendly.

Although he tended to shuffle along, the elder Mr. Williams looked to be in fair shape. He was of average build, and had a crown of gray hair surrounding a bald spot on the top of his speckled head. He looked dapper in a medium brown suit with a white long sleeved shirt, and a mauve and turquoise patterned tie. He had a violet pocket hanky protruding from his upper left breast pocket. The hanky was done in a crown fold pattern, a trick I've never been able to pull off.

Mrs. Williams was equally as chic and was dressed in a bright red textured suit with shoulder pads and shaping seams. Her matching skirt was tapered and had slits, and came down to just below her knee. Underneath, was a full collared blouse with a ruffled placket that was the color of butter. Topping off her ensemble was a satin feather floral sun hat in the same shade of red as her suit. It was perched atop a short, but thick head of ginger colored hair that may, or may not have been, a weave.

Dortell himself was escorting his grandmother and had his arm entwined in hers as he guided her up to the outside of the church. He was dressed in a simple black suit with a light teal shirt, and a silver tie. He looked no worse for wear considering his collapse on the field yesterday, and I couldn't help but think about the old Timex watch slogan: "Takes a lickin' and keeps on tickin'."

The Williams threesome stopped just outside the front door to the church and joined a small throng of other congregates, greeting them and conversing.

At about five minutes to ten, organ music, and then singing, began to emanate from the church's interior as the call to worship was made. The people clustered with the Williams family hurriedly checked their watches, and then realizing that God could not be kept waiting, disappeared en masse into the structure.

I had worn my Sunday best along with all of the faithful today and debated on whether or not I should enter the church and observe the service. Now, sitting here and hearing the first hymn wash through the parking lot like a wave, I realized that probably not much could be learned from going in and sitting through the service. Also, being the only white person within about two miles of here would be about as inconspicuous as an F-16 at a kite flying contest, and would probably draw undo attention to me—possibly from Dortell himself.

In the end, I decided to keep a low profile, give everyone a little privacy, and stay out in my car. It was a cool fall day and so I rolled down the windows, pulled out my laptop and began to catch up on some of the work I had been neglecting recently.

In many ways, being a blackmailer is a lot like other businesses and that's exactly how I ran it. My product was secrecy, and along with delivering my service to my 'clients' came the sundry details of functioning and making a profit. I had accounts payable for things like private mailboxes, mobile device carriers, re-mailing services, secure cloud servers, etc. And then of course there were my account receivables, which were payments from my many targets. Some of these required a gentle nudge from time to time, while others were so terrified of being exposed that they never missed a payment. But the extortion business wasn't evergreen, and sometimes payments inexplicably stopped altogether.

There wasn't always a nefarious motive at work here as time and circumstances changed that could quite rightfully allow people to decide that they no longer needed to pay for the taciturnity of One Eyed Jack.

For instance, a person that I might have been leaning on for infidelity might have gotten caught with his or her pants down anyway and had their marriages fall to pieces. Embezzlers, and others of their ilk, might get caught for another offense and get sent to the pokey. And sometimes, people simply died.

But I still had to investigate each of these prematurely delinquent accounts lest someone was attempting to pull a fast one on me—which occasionally happened. It took a lot of my attention following up with obituaries, arrest reports, and divorce documents and, then of course, the old accounts had to be replaced by new income streams. Hence my appearance here today.

I worked for about fifty minutes and was pleased with my productivity when I heard what sounded like it might have been recessional hymn booming out of the house of God. I shut down my laptop and stowed it. Rolled up the windows and stepped outside, grabbing my suit coat in the process.

I was still buttoning it up, and about halfway across the parking lot when first a couple of ushers, and then the minister himself glided out onto the front steps of the church. I watched as congregants spilled out behind him and formed a receiving line of sorts. There were more hearty handshakes, hugs, kisses, as well as laughter and smiles. It was a good time to have the spirit fill you.

I waited patiently as the Williams family came out and paid their proper respects to the minister before inserting themselves back into one of the pockets of people that had formed and began socializing.

I slowly stepped closer to the church until I was noticed by several of the congregants. I pointed to Dortell, and one of them reached over and tapped him on the shoulder, gesturing to me.

Dortell excused himself and broke off from the person he was talking to. I didn't want to get within earshot of the crowd of onlookers and stood my ground in the parking lot about fifty feet away from the church, waiting for him to intercept me.

When he was about ten feet from me, he said, "Can I help you sir?"

"Yes, I said. I think you might be able to."

He looked at me suspiciously and I gestured for him to come to my far side so that my back was to the church and any prying eyes. As soon as he was in place, I pulled my suit coat open, revealing the fake DEA badge that was hanging off of my belt.

Dortell glanced down at the badge and his eyes went a little wider, but he kept his composure well. Growing up in South LA as a black youth, he might have seen more than his share of law enforcement badges, sometimes for doing nothing more than walking down the street.

His gaze moved back up to my face.

"Jack Roberts, DEA," I said, when our eyes met. "I'd like to talk to you, and to make this as comfortable as possible for you."

He looked visibly upset, and trying to hold himself in check. "So that's why you followed me to church?" he said angrily under his breath. "So you could approach me in front of my whole family?"

"We would rather have not," I said, apologetically. "But you're a tough guy to get alone. Coach McCormick makes sure of that."

He stood there staring at me, processing what I said. Finally…

"So what's this about, Mr. Roberts?"

"Drugs, performance enhancing drugs to be specific."

He looked off into the distance and shook his head. When he turned back to me, he sighed the weary sigh of a man who had been proclaiming his innocence for too long.

"I don't juice," he insisted.

"Really?" I shot back, "And yet you can run faster than any one on that field, way faster than when you were playing high school ball. How do you explain that?"

"I said, I don't take anything," he said a little bit louder. His hand went up and he pointed to the church behind us. "I'd say I swear to it, but we're at the Lord's house and I won't do that."

"Is everything okay here?"

The sound came from behind me, a booming baritone voice. I turned and saw that it was Dortell's grandfather, Henry.

It could have been an awkward moment, but before the UCLB running back was forced to explain my unexpected presence, I came to his rescue.

"No problem, Mr. Williams," I said breezily. "I'm with the local paper and just wanted to get a few words from Dortell about yesterday's game. He's a tough one to get a hold of, and I'm on a deadline. I hope you don't mind."

"Oh, okay," he said easily and then smiled a nice smile. He had a mouth of teeth that were as big as a horse's.

Still smiling his giant toothy grin, the elder Williams turned back to his grandson and said, "I'll take your grandma home, Dortell." and then he headed back towards the front steps of the church.

When his grandfather had gotten far enough away, Dortell said softly, "Thanks. I appreciate that."

"No problem. Like I said; I want this to be comfortable for you and that means private. We can keep this just between you and me if you want, Dortell. No one else. Not your family, the coaches, the media, or the other players, you understand?"

"Yes sir," he said. "I can keep a secret."

"Good."

As he watched his grandmother and grandfather shuffle off the church property and head home, he changed gears, explaining to me his familial situation, which I didn't reveal to him that I was already privy to.

"They raised me," he said. "Since I was a little kid. My mom, well, she had some problems, and she died when I was eleven."

I nodded sympathetically, and didn't raise the issue of his wayward father. It was probably equally as painful, and was an all too familiar problem in the African American community.

"And they raised me right," he added proudly. "Even took me on a church mission with them to the Philippines when I was sixteen."

"Quite an adventure for a young man," I offered.

"It was—or rather it started out to be. I got real sick while I was there, and had to have emergency surgery for a ruptured gallbladder."

"Not exactly the kind of place I would want to have emergency medical treatment," I said.

"It wasn't. We were way out in the countryside, and didn't have access to a hospital. But it turned out that the Lord was watching out for me."

"Oh?" I said. "How so?"

"Doctors Without Borders," Dortell explained. "Luckily, there was a group of them working in a small clinic they had set up. They patched me up real good. But I still had to cut my trip short and fly home to recuperate. I really want to go back some day and continue the work that our mission started."

"I'm sure you will, Dortell," I said hopefully. "I'm sure you will."

We stood there staring at each other for a long time. If Dortell was snowing me, I couldn't detect it, and I didn't need to see his nose grow to smell bullshit.

"I don't take drugs, Mr. Roberts," he said finally. "And I don't need drugs. All I need is him."

"Who's that?" I asked.

Dortell Williams pointed beyond me and toward the church building

"The Lord, Mr. Roberts. All I need is the Lord."

TWENTY-TWO

I offered Dortell a ride to his house, but he politely refused and said that he wanted to walk home to sort out his thoughts. I could understand that.

I started up my car and began to head out of the parking lot. It had emptied somewhat, but there were still a few stragglers left.

From the exit of the lot, I couldn't cross straight over Central Avenue to head southbound, back to the freeway, so I turned right and headed northbound up the street to make a U-turn to get me back to the freeway.

As soon as I exited the lot, I spotted a white Dodge Challenger in my rearview mirror, pulling away from the curb just outside the church property. It was also heading northbound on Central Avenue. It stayed behind me at a legal distance and matched my speed, which was just at about the limit. I attempted to see who was in the car, but the front window was heavily tinted and I couldn't see through it. I glanced down at the front of the car to get a look at the front plate, but there wasn't any. The hairs on my neck began to stand up and tingle.

I eased over into the center median and made my U-turn, watching as the car behind me caught up quickly and then followed suit.

I hadn't been tailed in a long time, and so I began to calculate my options. I was in an unfamiliar neighborhood and if someone was in fact following me, turning down the wrong street into a dead-end could lead to dire consequences. I had a Beretta Px4 subcompact on me in a shoulder holster, but I wanted to avoid getting myself into any situation where I had to shoot my way out.

Trying to outrun them by speeding away would also put me as well as the public at risk, and I didn't want to go down that rabbit hole. Besides that, if the muscle car was sporting a Hemi engine, I'd be no match for it anyway. That was okay as I knew that there were plenty of ways to skin a cat.

I activated the map feature on my car's display. After it booted up and I located my current position, I was able to get a bird's eye view of my situation.

If I continued straight southbound on Central, it would take me directly back to the freeway. I would be relatively safe on the freeway, but I really wanted to see if the car was a tail, and so I decided to take the long way back.

I turned right onto 114th street and headed west, paralleling the freeway. My newfound friend did the same.

At Clovis Avenue, I made a left and started heading south again. Ditto for the car behind me.

Just to seal the deal, I turned right onto Imperial Highway and began heading westbound, and so did my tail.

I didn't know who it was or what they wanted, and I couldn't rely on being one hundred percent sure that I could lose them. I might lose this car, but there could be several cars working in concert and communicating with each other. And in this day and age, a drone could be flying overhead watching my every move. I couldn't take any chances and gave a voice command to call Tiffany.

She answered after about four rings and sounded groggy.

"Hi baby," she said in a sleepy voice. "On your way home?"

I knew that she had a show last night and that she didn't get home until about three. I felt like a heel for calling her, but I didn't want to put her into harm's way and put into action a plan that we had rehearsed several times previously.

"Not yet," I said and glanced in the rear view mirror. The white challenger was still there. "I've got some problems and I need you to bug out. The plan that we rehearsed."

"What?" she cried, suddenly coming awake. "What do you mean, Jack?"

"I'm being tailed," I said. "I'm sure of it. And I can't guarantee that I'll be able to shake them off completely, so you need to get out, just like we planned it."

"Oh Jack," she whimpered. "Are you sure?" Could it be a mistake?"

I could tell she was awake now, but she was also scared.

"Yes, I'm sure," I said confidently. "You have to do it Tiffany, alright?

"Alright Jack."

"Good. I'm going to put you on hold for a second," I said. "And activate the safe room camera so I can watch you."

A few seconds later, a darkened image came on car's display. It was from a CCTV camera that was mounted in the safe room in our house. The room was hidden under the elevator and could only be accessed by entering a special code into the security system. The code overrode the normal elevator controls by sending it to the second floor, while simultaneously opening the first floor door.

I got Tiffany back on and I could hear by her breathing that she was moving about.

"I'm back baby," I said. "What's going on?"

"Putting on my clothes," she said.

"Okay, good," I said, trying to sound upbeat and not believing my own voice for a second. I looked in the mirror and saw the Challenger keeping pace with me. I had almost a full tank of gas and could keep him at bay for quite a while, as long as I didn't take any wrong turns and get trapped.

"Don't rush baby," I said. "You've got plenty of time."

"Got my clothes and shoes on," she said. "I'm punching in the code into the security system now."

On my display in the car I saw the room flicker and then become illuminated. Inside of it were several guns safes as well as shelves that contained water, food, batteries, and two small backpacks known as 'bug out bags.' The bags were for a rapid escape from a situation, and each contained: identical handguns, spare clips and ammo, several thousand dollars in various denominations, fake driver's licenses and passports with clean credit cards to match, two untraceable Blackphones, six burner pre-paid cell phones complete with spoof cards, as well as first aid kits, some water, toiletries, and undergarments.

I watched on the screen as Tiffany descended the ladder into the safe room and began reaching for her backpack. She had her cell phone and her hands-free unit on.

"You remember what to do?" I said.

"Yeah," she said and slung the backpack over her shoulder before ascending back up the ladder. "I walk down to The Kettle Restaurant, making sure that no one is following me."

A few moments later, my display went dark as the Tiffany reset the security code to normal.

"Right," I said, "Then what?"

"I sit down and order a cup of coffee, and then call on the burner to have Adewale pick me up in a taxi. Correct?"

"Yes," I said, thankful that Tiffany had remembered the drill and most importantly, was cool under fire.

Adewale Abdul Okeke was a hard charging Nigerian refugee who ran a fleet of bandit taxis that operated illegally throughout the City of Angels. There were sets of magnetic signs with the names of competing taxi companies inside each of his vehicles. When another company's call was intercepted, the driver would slap the appropriate placards on the side of his taxi, race over to the pick-up, and snatch the customer before the requested company could earn a legitimate fare.

I had all the goods on him and called on him for loans of his vehicles as well as emergency pickups like this. It was a small price for him to pay for my silence, and he never complained or pushed back; after all, he had enough to worry about with Uber and Lyft eating his lunch on a daily basis.

"And where are you going to have him take you?" I prompted.

"To the Hilton by the airport where I just stay out of sight and wait for you to contact me."

I stole another glance at the car behind me and saw that it was still there.

"And what do you assume if I don't contact you in seventy-two hours?" I said.

"I assume that you're dead Jack," she said very quietly.

"Right. I love you, Tiffany."

"I love you too, Jack. Be careful."

TWENTY-THREE

I disconnected the call and returned to my task at hand. The Challenger was still back there and practicing typical tail pursuit tactics; putting another car between us, moving over a lane, but always with enough wiggle room to not lose me. As an old hand at this I knew that if they suddenly broke off, my worries would only be beginning as it meant I had been handed off to another—or possibly, several other cars.

I also knew that it was oft times better to not tip your hand by letting your tail know that you were aware of them, and so other than my series of illogical turns a couple of miles back, I maintained an illusion of blissful ignorance.

With Tiffany out of harm's way, I could now concentrate on the real task at hand: lose the tail and in the process, find out who was behind it. I voiced dialed one of my many valuable resources, and hoped he wasn't sitting in a jail cell or dead in the trunk of a car somewhere.

Tequan Sheshawn Tower was a South Los Angeles street criminal who ran in all the wrong circles, or the right ones depending on your needs or perspective. I called on him occasionally for various tasks that either went right to the edge of the law, or blatantly crossed straight over it. Thankfully, he answered after a couple of rings, knowing that it was me, and that my calls usually meant a good payday.

"Hey Jack, wus' up?" he said.

"I need a favor. You know any crews that do swoop and squats?"

A 'swoop and squat' was a term coined by the insurance companies after it became apparent to them that with California's lawsuit happy culture, money could be made by actually staging accidents against 'target' cars to collect big settlements. The most common method is to use a 'squat' car that is stuffed with passengers who have been paid by a person known as 'the capper', to perform the feat of slamming on their brakes in order to get rear-ended and claim fake injuries. In order to make the story more plausible; a swoop car is usually involved. After the squatter positions their car in front of the target vehicle, the other vehicle swoops in and hits their brakes, making the squat car's story believable.

"Shit yeah, when you need em?"

"Now. I've got a tail I want to lose. But I can play the swoop if that helps. I only need a squat."

"Hmmm, that could be kinda rough on such short notice," he said lazily, which I knew was code-speak for 'only if the money is right.'

"Would five grand smooth things up?" I asked. "You handle the splits."

"Oh yeah," he said brightly.

"Great. They can keep whatever they collect from insurance too; I just want the car stopped, and the driver's info and the VIN."

"You got it. Where's this all go'n down?"

"You tell me," I said. "I'm on Imperial Hwy westbound. I can see the 110 freeway up ahead. You tell me which way to go on it, north or south?"

"Imperial and the 110?" he cried incredulously. "What's your honky white ass doin' in the hood man?"

"Long story," I said. "Now which way, north or south? I gotta make a decision here soon."

Tequan thought for a moment before saying, "South, you's headin into Pedro. I got me some peeps in Wilmington that can hook up wicha there."

"Okay, south bound to Pedro it is."

I flipped on my blinker and moved over to pick up the southbound entrance ramp. Not shockingly, so did my white shadow.

Tequan then said, "Gotta put you hold for a bit and contact my boys."

"Got it, I'll be here."

I heard a click as I was put on hold. I turned onto the ramp for the southbound 110, or Harbor Freeway, to San Pedro. After I had safely merged and was in the number two lane, I used the touch screen to log my destination. I didn't know what the traffic was going to be like and wanted to give Tequan's co-conspirators an ETA so they could plan accordingly.

I checked the mirror and saw that the Challenger was one lane over in the number three lane and about one hundred and fifty feet behind me. This guy was patient, and I didn't like that.

Tequan came back on a few moments later.

"Take the Harbor all the way to the end and merge onto Gaffey Street and keep driving south. They'll pick you up at around first, and the shit will go down around third or so, depending on traffic. Call me back when you a couple of minutes out, and I'm gonna put you onto them in a conference call."

"Will do," I said, and Tequan hung up.

The drive south on the 110 was uneventful and the Challenger matched my speed and stayed put in the number three lane. After we passed the Pacific Coast Highway exit, the Challenger moved over to my lane. I dialed Tequan.

"I'm a couple of miles away from Gaffey," I said.

"Cool," he said. "Stand by."

I was put on hold for a second and then heard another voice come on the line, in the background I could hear street sounds and imagined them sitting just off of Gaffey Street, which was a main thoroughfare through the city of San Pedro.

Tequan came back on.

"Jack, meet my man Lester."

"Hey Lester," I said.

"S'up?" he said groggily. "What kinda ride you in?"

"Silver 2016 Honda Pilot. Need a plate number?"

"Nah. We sittin at Sepulveda and Gaf. Who do you want cracked? What kinda car?"

"White Dodge Challenger."

I looked up and saw that my tail was now directly behind me. “He’s right behind me and we’re turning south onto Gaffey as soon as the light changes. We’ll be in the middle lane.”

“Kay. I got you. We pick you up as soon as you turnin’.”

“Got it.”

The light changed and a cluster of cars turned left onto Gaffey Street south.

At Sepulveda and Gaffey, I saw an older model Camry sitting and waiting patiently, the car had at least five people crammed into it in order to maximize the number of fake injuries for settlement payments. It turned right and started following the Challenger and myself as soon as we drove by.

“I gotcha,” Lester said. “Just stay in that lane and do what I tells ya.”

“Right,” I said.

We passed First Street and in my rear view mirror, I saw Lester’s Toyota cut in and merge with traffic. It cut over to the left-hand lane and accelerated to catch up with us.

"Just stay where you at," Lester said. "But at some point, I gonna have you move up a bit so we can squeeze in for the squat."

"Got it," I said and saw that the Camry was about even with the Challenger. It moved up to where it was just about even with me.

"You need me to tap my brakes when you cut in?" I asked.

Yeah, Lester said and then a moment later said. "Okay, move up about thirty feet. As soon as we in, tap you brakes."

"Will do."

As instructed, I accelerated and gave them the room they needed to work. The Camry swerved into the space I created and I did a quick light tap on the brakes, just enough to have the lights come on, but not enough to slow me to cause an actual rear-ender.

The Camry slammed on its brakes and I heard the screech of tires followed by the crunching of metal and glass breaking. Behind it, I could see the Challenger slightly askew as the driver had tried to avoid the collision. I accelerated just enough to put some distance between myself and the accident, and started to mentally work out my route home.

I turned right onto Third Street which I thought I could use to double back to Gaffey at First and then jump back onto the 110 freeway north to take me home. But Third Street was a dead end and I would have to turn around. I started to veer off to the right to give me room for a wide U-turn, and then I heard a voice cry out from the phone. It wasn't the message I wanted to hear.

"Shit, man!" Lester said. "Mother-fucker took off. He's going after you ass!"

TWENTY-FOUR

"Damn it!"

I was halfway through the U-turn when I saw the Challenger skid around the corner and come roaring up the street after me. The right front side of the car was caved in and the bumper was hanging crazily to one side, but it was still drivable.

I held the wheel hard to the left and punched the accelerator, hoping to turn around in time to get out, but the Challenger careened up and wedged me in. The passenger side door flew open and a large Asian man bolted out of the car. He had a suppressed pistol in his hand.

I saw a puff of smoke emerge from the end of the suppressor and my driver's side window exploded in a shower of glass a nanosecond later.

Instinctively, I recoiled and closed my eye to avoid getting hit by the glass. Simultaneously, I began to reach for the Beretta in my shoulder holster. Before I could retract it, I felt the still warm end of the suppressor jammed against my temple.

"Hands!" his voice commanded, and I knew it would be suicide at this point to try to do anything but comply; these guys knew what they were doing.

I pulled my right hand away from my jacket slowly, and with fingers splayed, placed it on the steering wheel along with my left.

The driver of the Challenger, another Asian, had emerged now and ran up next to the shooter. With the gun still held to my head, the driver reached in and cuffed my hands together with a set of zip tie restraints. Then he switched off the ignition and pulled a syringe out of his pocket. Before I could try to resist, the driver stabbed it into my neck it and depressed the plunger. In a few seconds, I was off to dreamland.

* * *

I woke up a couple of hours or days later to the drone of a motor running. I was lying on my back and felt the dubious comfort of a thin mattress underneath me. It was warm, but not wet from sweat. I tried to move my arms, but my hands were cuffed behind me. They were going numb, but I could still feel enough to recognize that my restraints were the plastic tie wrap variety. They were easy enough to get out of if you knew how, and more importantly, nobody was watching. But I still didn't know what my situation was, so I opened my eye and started to access things.

Above me was a ceiling the color of a brick; it was corrugated and appeared to be made of metal. An LED light fixture illuminated the space over my bed. I rolled my head from side to side and saw that the two walls on either side of me were of the same material and color. I knew then that I was being held inside a cargo container.

I lifted my head and looked toward the far end of the container, away from my bed. A wall of thick mesh wire divided the container roughly in half. The mesh wall hung on hinges on one side and was secured with two hasps and heavy duty locks on the other side. Beyond the wall were the heavy doors of the container and an AC unit that was humming away.

The only furniture on my side of the container behind the wire mesh was my bed, and a port-a-potty unit. An unopened bottle of water sat on the floor next to the bed along with an unopened roll of toilet paper and a container of anti-bacterial wipes. On the other side of the mesh was a couple of plastic patio chairs, and high up in the corner, a video camera aimed in the direction of my makeshift cell. The red light was illuminated on the front face and I imagined I was being monitored.

I noted that my clothes had been removed and I had been dressed in a pair of sweatpants and a T-shirt. I had no belt and my shoelaces had been removed, standard procedure when a prisoner is on suicide watch. Based on what I could feel through my clothes and against my skin, my phone, my jewelry, and all of my IDs, both fake and legitimate, had been taken from me. Again, par for the course in inmate management.

I rolled off of the bed and stood up. My body was stiff. I didn't know how long I had been here or what time it was, but there was one way every post-pubescent man could try to estimate the passing of time; I rubbed my cheek against the shoulder of my T-shirt to try to estimate how much my beard had grown. I guessed it to be about a day's worth.

I heard a loud screech coming from the end of the container as the levers that held the doors closed were being lifted and turned. I stood up.

One of the doors opened up and I could see that it was daytime. That was about all I could see though, as beyond the door was nothing more than a cinder block wall. It was who stepped through the door though that really gave me pause.

"Hello Jack," Chris Moore said.

TWENTY-FIVE

"Mother-fucker," I cursed under my breath.

The newspaper reporter stepped further into the container, followed by the enormous Asian man who had shot out my car window. The big man pulled the heavy door closed behind him and then stood by with sentry-like crossed arms and eyed me warily. An automatic pistol was shoved into a holster under his muscled arm and he reminded me vaguely of the character, *Odd-Job*, from the early James Bond films.

"You just can't stop lying to me, can you Jack?" Moore said as he got within a few feet of the wire mesh of my makeshift cell. "First, you were a struggling journalist on the sports beat, and then an undercover DEA agent. I can't decide whether you're a real-life Pinocchio, or Walter Mitty." He laughed at his own joke.

"How do you know I'm not with DEA?" I said, trying to sound cagey.

"Because the people I work for know how to check these things out. The phony journalist story was easy, but the DEA line required deeper resources, so I turned to my employer."

"And who might that be?" I asked.

"In due time," Moore said absently while picking a piece of lint from his shirt. He was dressed in a pair of light gray chinos and a dark red long sleeved sateen shirt with a tie the color of a tangerine. I shifted on my feet, realizing my bladder was full and I would need to empty it soon.

"Well if you won't tell me the *who*," I said. "Then at least tell me the why. Was it because I was getting a little too close to your dope empire?

"Dope? Not dope Jack, not in the conventional sense anyway. Something much better than that, as you will soon see."

I nodded mutely, and decided to get the inevitable out of the way.

"All right," I said evenly. "So when do you kill me, or are you going to torture me first?"

"No torture," my host said, "At least not of the variety most people think of. As far as your death, that will be up to you and how long your body will endure. For now though, you will be well taken care of. In fact, we want you to stay very healthy."

I was about to ask why, when there was a knock on the door of the cargo container, more like a dull thud than anything. The big Asian guard pushed the heavy door open a crack to see who it was, and then shoved it open wider to allow his cohort in my abduction and a much smaller man to enter. The small man was Asian as well and was about seventy years old with thinning hair on a shiny pate that was dotted with age spots. He was dressed in a white lab coat with a stethoscope hanging from his neck and was carrying a small black duffel bag and a clipboard. He was wearing thick plastic framed glasses that were ill-fitting as they continually slid down his nose, and he shuffled from the end of the container towards the cage door with a noticeable stoop to his posture.

Moore and the doctor acknowledged each other silently, and then he and the large man continued walking toward the cage I was being held in.

When they reached it, the larger man produced a set of keys and got to work on the two padlocks that held it closed.

When they were both unlocked, he swung the big gate open, its hinges squealing in protest, and the two of them entered.

“The doctor is going to give you a brief physical exam, Jack,” Chris Moore said, turning to me. “Just to see if you are up to the task we have planned for you.”

“And what task is that?” I asked.

Moore remained mum and sat down on one of the plastic chairs on his side of the container, straightening the creases in his chinos. The doctor emptied the contents of his bag out onto the bed. I saw a portable blood pressure cuff, a digital thermometer, an otoscope, stethoscope, clean syringes, latex gloves, tongue depressors—essentially all of the tools needed for a physician to give you the once over, a once over for what I just didn't know.

I looked over at Moore.

"Can I take a leak first?" I asked. "Before we start this?"

He considered it for a moment, then shook his head and said, "No, this won't take long—if you cooperate. Then you can pee."

I took a deep breath and gritted my teeth, which I felt were going to start floating in my mouth before long. I wondered what the big deal was, keeping me in restraints with about eight hundred pounds of beef guarding me.

As the big man stood guard inside the cage, the doctor silently went through the steps to check out my state of health. He checked my blood pressure (which was elevated—but whose wouldn't be), my pulse, my ears, nose, and throat. Two samples of blood were taken from my right arm and I had my lungs and my prostate checked. I was even stripped and checked for a hernia. Each vital sign was logged onto a form on a clipboard.

While he was going through all of this, I was able to steal a glance at the entries on the paper on his clipboard and noted that they were written in logograms, or Chinese characters.

The exam apparently concluded, the doctor pushed his glasses up on his nose for about the fiftieth time and turned toward Chris Moore.

"Okay," he said in halting English.

"Hǎo," Moore nodded, smiling."Jìxù"

I recognized the language as Chinese, but had no idea about what was being said. The translation would soon become apparent though as the doctor motioned to the bigger man who came around behind me and grabbed me, pinning my arms to my side.

"What the fuck!" I yelled at the guard then turned toward Moore. "I'm cooperating with the old sawbones here! What's the fucking problem? What more do you need?"

"DNA," Moore said casually. "We already have your blood, but we need some more samples from you."

"Samples for what?"

"For the crime scene, Jack."

"What crime scene?" I wanted to say, when the doctor suddenly produced a gouge chisel, used by craftsmen for scooping wood out of a board.

The doctor twisted my head sideways as the big guy held me still. The doctor was surprisingly strong for his diminutive size, and held the sharp curved point of the chisel against my cheek. He dug it in and scrapped it roughly across my skin, cutting into it.

"Aaggh!" I screamed as I felt blood beginning to trickle down my face. "Fuck you, you fucking bastards!"

The doctor very carefully scraped the skin into a small vial and then returned the chisel to my face for round two.

This time I put up a bigger fight and began turning my face from side to side rapidly. The doctor couldn't get a grip on me and looked up desperately at the hulk pinning my shoulders.

The big man released one of his arms from around me and grabbed a fist full of my hair from the top of my head; he twisted it and pulled my head so far sideways against my shoulder I thought it was going to snap off. The doctor proceeded to take more samples.

At this point, I lost all control of my bladder and it released. I felt a flood of warm liquid issue forth in my crotch.

After the doctor had put three furrows into the side of my face, he glanced one more time at the big man who was holding me and nodded. The big man ripped a mass of hair from my head and then released me.

I fell back onto the bed and watched as the big man dropped my hair into a baggie provided by the doctor.

The doctor swabbed my face with an alcohol wipe and affixed a large bandage over my wounds.

After all, if they wanted to keep me healthy for whatever they had in mind, they couldn't risk infection.

He picked up his instruments and placed everything back into the duffel as if it were just one more routine house call. Which for him, it might have been. Then he turned to look at me, pushed his glasses up one more time, and for some reason, nodded.

He stepped out of the cell and handed the Vacutainer tube containing my blood, as well as the skin and hair samples to Chris Moore, along with the medical form.

"Xièxiè," Chris Moore said, and then the doctor and the second goon departed.

With me subdued, Moore dragged his plastic chair into the cell and set it next to my bed so he was facing me. He turned toward the monster guarding the door and nodded.

The big man stepped forward into my end of the container and with a flash, produced a Kershaw Launch 3 fully automatic knife and clicked it open. He pulled me up off the bed like I weighed nothing, spun me around backward, and cut off my plastic restraints. The monster guarding me took a few steps back, but remained standing there, ever vigilant and ready to pounce on an instant's notice.

"Sorry about that Jack," Moore said, gesturing to my wetted crotch. "We'll get you some new clothes soon."

I looked over at him and wanted to lunge out and strangle him, but I knew that that was a primal reaction, and that of all the assets a man has: his back, his balls and his brains, the smart warrior knows that sometimes patience is golden. At this point, I had to remain cool and hope that an opportunity for escape would come my way. But first I wanted to know about my fate.

"So what fucking crime scene are you placing my DNA at?" I practically spat at him.

Chris Moore smirked back at me and then said flatly, "Why the one where you kill Ken McCormick, Jack."

TWENTY-SIX

I stared at him for a long time, trying to process it; but there were too many crazy things happening, and the cast of this tragic comedy were in a constant state of flux. Allies became enemies and vice-versa. I felt like I was stuck in a cross between the Mad Hatter's Tea Party and a Fellini movie.

"So, you're going to kill Ken McCormick and frame me for it?" I said.

"Yes," Chris Moore said, as casually as if I asked him if he was going to change the oil on his car.

"Why, I hardly even know Mr. McCormick," I said sarcastically. "Why would I want to kill him?"

"Because he was having sexual relations with a woman that you were trying to score with. Classic jealous rage—at least that's what it will look like when the police investigate. He has a problem with pussy, in case you didn't know. And that's his downfall."

I didn't let on that I was aware of the offensive coordinators previous dalliances.

"And so you will bludgeon Mr. McCormick to death after you learn that he has had relations with your woman," Moore continued. "It will be a crime of passion, and he will struggle."

I rubbed the bandage on my cheek where the doctor had scraped the skin out. My scalp was still smarting from having the hair pulled out. I nodded.

"And then my hair, my blood, and even my skin will be all over the crime scene, correct?"

Chris Moore nodded and smiled. He was proud that it had been planned so completely. "You catch on well Jack; I'll say that for you."

I let out a big breath of air and stared at him. As much as I wanted to try to make a run for it and take my chances, I knew they were nil. But knowledge was power, and if Moore was going to get loose lipped on me because of his ego, then I'd try to keep pumping him until it petered out.

"Was McCormick working for you?"

"Yes."

"Did he come to you, or did you guys go to him?" I asked.

"You could say that we approached Mr. McCormick and made him an offer he couldn't refuse." Moore said evasively.

I nodded, realizing then that McCormick had been turned by Moore and his cohorts, whoever they may be. It was an easy enough scenario to envision; they setup an attractive woman to come on to him during a road game, McCormick and the chippy have a little toss in the hay, and then the video comes out, along with a simple deal to keep it from Mrs. McCormick. It was classic Femme Fatale 101.

"So why is he being killed?" I asked. "What exactly did he do to become the sacrificial lamb?"

"He almost killed Dortell Williams is what he did," Moore said.

"What!" I said incredulously. "How? Did he give him an overdose of the juice you're putting into Dortell? You want to tell me what the hell is going on here, Moore?"

My captor regarded me silently for a moment and then said, "Sure, why not. You'll know soon enough, Jack."

I waited and watched as he took in a big breath of air and then let it out, as if he had a long story to tell. He stood up and started to pace the floor in front of me, but only after he checked his shirt and pants for any stray pieces of lint again. Finding none, he began.

"Ken McCormick was working for us on a special project" he said.

"Who's us?" I asked.

"The CAA, or Chinese Athletic Association."

"And what exactly does the Chinese Athletic Association have to do with a US College football player and his coach?" I asked.

Chris Moore turned to me and smiled.

He said, "Because the ambitions and reach of Beijing are long, Jack. And because of that, Americans are now China's guinea pigs."

TWENTY-SEVEN

I let what Moore had just confessed sink in. The mystery of Dortell's incredible ability on the playing field was beginning to take shape. Moore and McCormick were somehow complicit in the juicing of Dortell. But Dortell was adamant that he wasn't doping and, unlike most people who cross my path, I believed him. He certainly didn't seem crazy enough to willingly become a lab rat for The People's

Republic. He was either really stupid and a great liar, or they were somehow feeding him drugs without his knowledge. I would bet money that it was the second scenario.

“So are you feeding Dortell Williams performance enhancing drugs without his knowledge?” I asked.

“No. No drugs,” Moore replied. “Drugs are passé; our organization learned that lesson from Russia’s ban in the Rio Olympics. This is a new era. We are just controlling what Mr. William’s body produces naturally.

“Produces naturally,” I repeated. “Like what, his testosterone?”

Moore turned toward me and stopped.

“No. His adrenaline, Jack. We are in control of Mr. William’s adrenal gland.”

I shook my head in disbelief. “You’re kidding?”

Chris Moore shook his head and continued.

“Mr. Williams has a device installed in him that can stimulate his adrenal gland to release adrenaline. It isn’t a new concept actually. The

Israelis did some work in this area a few years ago, but the device that they created only releases adrenaline that has been preloaded into the body to deal with chronic medical issues, much like an insulin pump does for diabetes. Our scientists took the concept further by creating a device that stimulates the adrenal gland through electrical signals."

"Similar to what a pacemaker does for the heart," I offered.

"Exactly."

"And let me guess, since adrenaline is a natural substance produced by the body, it doesn't show up on any drug tests?"

"Correct."

"Does Dortell know that he has this device in him?" I asked.

"No. He's completely unaware of it. He thinks he just an incredibly gifted athlete—which maybe deep down, he really is."

"So how did he come about to have this device put in him without his knowledge?"

"Several years back he had emergency surgery in the Philippines on his gallbladder. It was close enough to his adrenal gland that it was simple matter of installing it then."

I thought back to Dortell had told me about his medical history, by way of his aborted church mission in the Philippines. And it was foreign doctors that were there on a humanitarian mission that worked on him.

"Chinese doctors," I offered. "From Doctors Without Borders?"

"Yes," Moore went on. "The CAA had gone over there with the device and was hoping to find a healthy young boy to put it in, maybe offer his destitute family some money. But the children of the PI are not a healthy lot, and we weren't sure if we could expect the level of performance we were trying to achieve. When Dortell was brought in for emergency surgery, the CAA thought he would make a much better candidate. He's fit, healthy, and he plays in a public sport where it would be easy to monitor his performance. We basically 'turbocharged' his body."

"You basically are running your own Tuskegee Study," I shot back, referring to the notorious medical program in 1932 that held back treatment for syphilis in black men.

Although he tried not to show it, being African American himself, the comment rattled Moore, and I watched gleefully as his Adam's apple bobbed in his narrow neck a couple of times.

"So where does McCormick fit into all of this?" I continued to press. "If he's not feeding Dortell any dope, and this thing is already in Dortell's body, what do you need him for?"

"He's the play caller and knows when to stimulate the adrenal gland. Plus, the release of adrenaline has to be measured and carefully controlled, or the body will go into shock from the overdose and eventually into cardiac arrest."

"Like the other day at the game when Dortell collapsed?" I suggested.

"Yes. That was Mr. McCormick's error."

I leaned back on the bed and rested on my elbows. The mattress was thin, but at least I wasn't sleeping on the floor, or shackled to a wall in a dungeon.

"So let me get this straight," I said. "Since McCormick knows the plays and when his running back will be getting the ball, you're using him to throttle this device to release the adrenaline at the optimum time to measure its performance."

"Exactly."

"How does he control it?"

"With his tablet device," Moore said as easily as if I were asking him how to send a text message. "Most of the coaches have them, to review plays and receive information from the booth and so forth. But McCormick's has a special program installed in his that remotely controls the electrical stimulation of the gland. It has a limited range, so it has to be close to the action to be effective."

"McCormick was the perfect man for the job," Moore went on. "But as I said; he got sloppy. And that is something we simply cannot tolerate. If a young, healthy man like Mr. Williams were to die unexpectedly on the field from the overdose of adrenaline, there would most certainly be an autopsy ordered."

"And then they would find the device," I said.

"Yes."

I stared down at the floor and thought about what Chris Moore had just revealed. McCormick almost blew the lid off of the whole thing by accidentally overdosing Dortell with adrenaline, and now they were going to relieve him of his duties. But just to make sure that he didn't spill the beans on Beijing's little lab rat experiment; they were going to kill him. But there was one thing I couldn't figure out. I looked back up at Moore.

"I get why you want to whack McCormick so he doesn't screw up your program again and then takes the secret to his grave," I said. "By why bother framing me for it? If you do a clean job, or make it look like an accident, there's no need to bring me into it."

Chris Moore smiled like he was going to pull the final rabbit out of the hat, and then he did.

"Because we have to have a reason for your disappearance, Jack," he said.

"Oh, I'm going to disappear." I said incredulously. "And just why, may I ask, do you have to have me disappear?"

“Because Dortell’s recent collapse was a wake-up call for my employers, and they need to see how much adrenaline the human body can withstand before it becomes terminal. And so, in a very short time, you’re going to be the CAA’s newest guinea pig,” Chris Moore said.

TWENTY-EIGHT

I stared at Moore as I began to appreciate the gravity of my dire situation. I was going to be sent—to God knows where—to have the adrenal stimulator device installed in me with the throttle pushed to the red line and beyond. I would be just like a lab rat making the ultimate sacrifice for science. And in the meantime, McCormick gets whacked with my DNA all over the crime scene. To anyone who looked at it, it would seem that I had done the dirty deed and then gone on the lam, never to return.

Moore smiled at me one last time as if this was going to be the perfect denouement to the program—which I had to admit it was—and then started out of my cage and to the door. He nodded to the hulking guard and the big man double locked the cage door. Together they started towards the door of the container.

"Dinner will be in an hour," Moore said over his shoulder. "Try to eat well and stay healthy. It will be much easier on you."

"The final meal of a condemned man?" I said.

"Something like that," Moore said breezily, and continued on.

When he was almost to the door of the container, he turned back at me and grinned.

"Oh, and will get you some new pants since you seemed to have wet your diaper in all the excitement," he teased.

"Fuck you!" I said.

He didn't respond, verbally or otherwise and the big lug pushed the heavy door open and they stepped out. It closed behind them and I heard the screech of the lever being operated and then the faint sound of a padlock clicking shut.

I lay back down on the bed and rubbed my eyes, chastising myself for pushing so hard to unravel the mystery of Dortell Williams when I just should have let sleeping dogs lie.

"Fuck!" I screamed. "Fuck, fuck, fuck!"

I thought of Tiffany as well and wondered how she was doing. Thankfully, I had gotten her out of the house and set into motion the exit plan I had devised for her. I knew that she would be fine from both a financial and security standpoint. And even though Moore and his band of thugs had my driver's license, the address listed on it went to a house that was nothing more than a mail drop that forwarded my personal mail through several other private drops. My car was registered in the name of a bogus company that was incorporated offshore through a Byzantine series of other companies. Trying to piece everything together just to find out where I lived or if I had any family to use as leverage against me would take a lot of effort and resources that they probably didn't care to expend. They had me now, their newest guinea pig, and that seemed to be their highest priority at this point. So what were their plans, I asked myself. And how was I going to throw a wrench into them?

Starting with the basics, I tried to figure out where I was, what time it was, discover any vulnerability in the setup of the container, and most importantly, try to think of a way to escape.

But could I do this with prying eyes constantly watching me? I didn't know for sure, but I had to err on the side of caution and assume that the camera trained on me would be monitored around the clock. That meant I couldn't be too aggressive in my probe of my surroundings, lest one of the supersized guards barge in and break me in half like I was a stale bread stick.

I looked at the overhead light above my bed and followed the conduit back to the only light switch in the room. Darn it; it was located far on the other side of the wire mesh door. Unless they shut it off for me to sleep—which I doubt they would—I could always count on the fact that they might be watching.

Still, there were other senses I could call on to analyze my predicament.

I listened for any sounds that might give away my location: traffic, train whistles, airplanes, but I couldn't hear anything above the noise of the AC unit. Whether my captors had thought of that by design or not, I couldn't say.

I didn't have a very good sense of smell, but still I tried to take a whiff to see if I could detect any distinctive odors, either aromatic or otherwise. I smelled nothing that would tell me that I was near a petrochemical facility, a meat packing plant, or a medical marijuana dispensary. They say that 'the nose knows' but not mine, or not today. So much for that idea.

I looked for gaps and cracks in the container to see sunlight, but there were none. I placed my hand on walls to feel heat of sun. It would help if I was going to be in here for a while to keep track of how many days had elapsed.

So far the surface was hottest on the top of the container, with the wall closest to my bed warmer than the one on the other side. Okay, One Eyed Jack, one cycle of this and you'd know what the orientation of the trailer was; big whoop for you. You still don't know where you are or how in the hell you're going to escape.

And lastly, I checked the integrity of the cage door itself. The frame was made of heavy angle iron and was welded, not bolted together and the wire mesh was welded to the frame. On top of that, the frame hinges and the hasps were all welded in. So even if I could fashion something that would work as a wrench or screwdriver, there were no fasteners to undo.

Even if I did, I could still be detected if they were watching the camera monitor and then I still would have to find a way to either get through the main door or possibly push through the air conditioning unit before they came charging in here.

I sat back down on the bed with my back against the wall, realizing that I wasn't going to be able to create an opportunity to escape and that I would just have to wait for them to give one to me. Whether or not that would occur or if I was just going to depart this dear earth as the failed human experiment of some corrupt nation state, just became the biggest question on my mind.

TWENTY-NINE

In prisons throughout the United States, solitary confinement is nicknamed, ‘The Hole’ and it’s an apt title. While not physically located below ground, your emotions and spirit certainly sink to unimaginable depths. Over the past several days and nights, I had engaged in the same behaviors that any prisoner who was confined and cut off from the world would partake in. I paced my cell endlessly, memorizing the dimensions exactly. I listened for sounds, occasionally even imagining some like the chirp of a bird, or a person singing. I examined and reexamined every single corner and crevice, looking for an opportunity. I was unsuccessful on each count.

But if I couldn't escape outright I reasoned, then maybe I could somehow derail the CAA's program some other way? The Chinese had taken the extra step to check my physical condition and Moore himself had stated that they wanted me to remain healthy. But what if I wasn't healthy enough to make me a viable candidate, and if so, how would I achieve this? They were feeding me three substantial meals per day at regular intervals, but what if I didn't eat them? I could go on a hunger strike and allow my body to become malnourished and emaciated.

I considered the possible outcomes of such a campaign to undermine my otherwise good physical condition, and in the end, determined that they wouldn't achieve my ultimate goal of escape. Granted, I would become damaged goods in my captor's eyes and derail or at least set back their program. But I would probably be summarily executed, dumped into a shallow grave in the Chinese countryside, and never heard from again. It would be a symbolic and final act of defiance, but it wouldn't get me out of here and back with Tiffany. As long as there was even the narrowest sliver of escape on the horizon, I knew that I needed to stay healthy.

When I wasn't on my clandestine snooping missions or fantasizing about ways to thwart the CAA's experiment, I speculated at length on Chris Moore's role in this whole thing, and how he had been enlisted to cooperate. His role seemed fairly straightforward and was common practice for authoritarian regimes. The Chinese weren't about to entrust McCormick with their experiment without having some oversight, and Moore with his press pass and access and knowledge of the UCLB organization, was a logical choice to play handler.

As far as how he got involved in the whole thing was something that had many different possibilities. He could have had a skeleton in the closet, and similar to McCormick been conscripted into joining the operation, but his actions didn't seem to jibe with this. He seemed to be too cocky and self-assured when he was lording over me in the cargo container, as if he was about to realize a big payday for his services.

I've known several writers and journalists in my day—and have even blackmailed a few of them. I know that they typically work long hours for low pay under grueling deadlines with no guarantee that it will lead to anything worthwhile in the end. Moore could have been approached by the CAA, offered a big carrot, and bit on it. But whether the reporter would ever realize it was another thing entirely. With McCormick out of the picture and my head—and everything connected to it—delivered to the scientists at the CAA on a silver platter, he might become excess baggage and could soon find himself meeting a more hasty demise than yours truly. I could only hope.

I thought about Jerry Pine as well, and kicked myself for focusing so much on him. I deduced that he probably didn't have any role in this nefarious experiment, and other than McCormick having to keep him away from Dortell, was a minor inconvenience. In the big picture of things, he might have even helped to keep the spotlight off the UCLB blue chip by supplying the dope that other players might someday be taken down by.

And lastly, I thought of my life, and of Tiffany, and of our life together: what it was, and what it could have become. But more than anything, I sat around and waited the wait of a condemned man.

* * *

Based upon my observations of the warmth of the walls indicating the passage of the sun and the fact that I had been served ten meals, I estimated that an additional four days had passed since I first came to. That put it at Friday evening, possibly close to midnight, based on the coldness of the container walls.

I was dozing when I heard the now familiar screech of the door being unlatched and opened. Behind it, the two guards that had been attending to me stepped inside. They walked toward the cage door and one of them unlocked it and came inside while the other kept a safe distance on the other side, his hand on his armament.

The one who stepped inside roughly jerked me off the bed and onto my feet. He handcuffed my wrists in the back with standard metal overlock police cuffs and started pulling me toward the opening at the far end. I recognized what was happening and my pulse began to race from either excitement or fear; I was being moved, and it was either going to be my only chance for escape, or it was the start to the countdown toward the end of my life.

We stepped through the opening and no matter what my fate held, it felt liberating just to be on the other side of the container at that moment in time. I sensed my surroundings, but rather than look around and examine them, I looked up to the sky instead.

A full moon was directly above us, its bright light washing out the stars and bathing the area around us with illumination. I took in a deep breath through my nostrils and the fresh night air tasted like heaven.

Behind me I heard the door being closed and latched. A heavy denim jacket was draped over my shoulders and the zipper was pulled up nearly to my neck, hiding my cuffed hands and offering an extra layer of restraint. One of the big men got in front of me and started to walk; the other one took up a position at my flank and prodded me to follow. We began walking in silence.

As I had suspected, the location I had been held for the past several days was in a remote industrial area. There were several other shipping containers set in neat rows along with some outbuildings, and overhead, high voltage power lines that buzzed and crackled. The moon's glow made it easy enough to see, but the surroundings had a muted colorless hue to them. Everything was varying shades of gray. The ground beneath us was dirt and gravel, and it kicked up clouds of fine dust as we walked. A feral cat became spooked and darted out from the side of one of the containers, causing the guard in front of me to instinctively reach for his gun. Not only were these guys big, they were alert and fast.

I was led to a dark colored, windowless van parked next to a decrepit shed made of corrugated metal. The first man opened the back door while the other one gagged my mouth with a bandana and tied it in a tight knot behind my head.

I was shoved into the back of the van and fell down on the hard metal interior floor. The man flanking me got in as well and sat down on a plastic milk crate next to me. He put his foot on my back as an indicator that I was to stay down. The back door slammed shut and the other man got in the front to drive.

Absent in all of this was my erstwhile friend and confidant, Chris Moore. Maybe he had already reached his expiration date and was now in a shallow grave somewhere. If so, I could only hope it was a painful demise.

We drove for about twenty minutes with barely a word being passing between the two men. I noted that the driver took a direct route and didn't engage in the endless turns one direction and then the other, designed to disorient and confuse a captive. They obviously weren't worried about me knowing where we were going. My guess was because it was a one-way trip.

When we finally came to a stop, I noticed the inside of the van was pulsing with the reflections of some external strobe. Then I heard the distinctive whine of a turbine engine coming up to speed and realized we were at an airport.

The rear van doors were opened and I was dragged out again. This time I took a look around and saw that we were on the tarmac at the Hawthorne Airport, a small municipal airport that served every type of aircraft from the simplest of single engine prop planes, to private jets and helicopters.

To the south of us was the huge manufacturing plant of SpaceX, brainchild of the visionary Elon Musk, and home of the revolutionary Falcon 9 rocket and the Dragon spacecraft. I looked over to the outside of the plant in hopes of spying some personnel that I could get the attention of, but everyone on the night shift must have been inside. Ditto for the trending restaurant Eureka, which served a great assortment of burgers and craft beers. It was dark and had already shuttered its doors for the evening. What I wouldn't give to be in there right now, hoisting a cold one and dining with Tiffany.

I was led towards a Hughes 500 helicopter sitting about two hundred feet from where we parked the van. The turbine was at idle speed and the rotor blades of the 500 were already spinning, creating a down-blast of air surrounding it. Inside, the pilot—who appeared to be another Chinese—was going through motions of checking his instrument and controls.

Just then, Chris Moore appeared from the far side of the helicopter. Fastidious as always, he was dressed in a pair of dark slacks and a lighter V-neck sweater the color of which I couldn't get an exact read on. When he saw us, he lowered his head and jogged toward us.

"Jack!" he yelled over the whine of the helicopter's turbine. "So glad you could make it."

I couldn't respond and Moore made a motion for the guards to remove my gag.

"I wouldn't miss it for the fucking world," I remarked back, when I was able to.

Moore smiled the smile of a man laying down a winning poker hand and said, "So sorry I can't accompany you, but I've got a game to catch. The Dolphins are playing the Cal Bears up north, and it's supposed to be a great contest. I just wanted to wish you bon voyage before you took off. It's been a pleasure knowing you, Jack."

He started to chuckle and I realized I couldn't stand his smugness any longer. If I was going out, I was going to do it with one final act of defiance. I activated my salivary glands and built up a big mouthful of spit. I was going to let loose on his face—as is customary—but then thought better of it and decided to hit him where it really hurt. I let loose with a huge lougey all over his nice sweater.

Moore instantly recoiled and let out a shriek that sounded like a little girl. The big lug that was in front of me, swung around and punched me in the gut. The blow doubled me over and took my breath away, but it was worth every bit of discomfort just to watch Chris Moore in a state of panic, desperately trying to wipe away the spit with his handkerchief. The way he was behaving, you would have thought I had doused him with acid.

The lug who hit me wound up for number two, but Moore stopped him, albeit, reluctantly.

"Don't!" he said to the monster, his hands busy trying to clean himself up. "Don't damage the goods. We need him as healthy as possible."

Then he turned to me and hissed, "Don't worry Jack; you'll get yours in the end—and I'll have the last laugh."

I pantomimed like I was going to spit again and I had the satisfaction of watching Moore jump back from me like I was a coiled rattlesnake about to strike. Then he nodded to the two goons and turned and walked away from the helicopter, his hands still wiping the front of his sweater.

My jacket was removed, and I was set into place in left rear seat directly behind the pilot. The handcuffs were opened momentarily and then re-latched in front of me through the grab bar on the back of the pilot's seat.

The rear door to the helicopter was closed, and the man who had ridden in the back of the van with me climbed into the seat next to the pilot and pulled on a pair of headphones. He said a few words to the pilot that I couldn't hear above the sound of the engine and they shook hands genially.

The driver of the van slapped his hand against the side glass and waved goodbye before lowering his head and jogging off back to the van.

I heard the whine of the turbine as the RPM increased and a few seconds later, we lifted off into the night sky.

THIRTY

As soon as we were able to clear it, the pilot banked the aircraft towards the south and we flew over the top of the SpaceX plant with just a dozen or so feet to spare. We continued heading due south for a short distance in order to avoid the LAX restricted airspace, and then turned west toward the Pacific Ocean.

When we got to the ocean just a few minutes later, the pilot turned south and hugged the coastline towards the Palos Verdes Peninsula. I saw beachfront houses off to my left, some with lights burning from inside and I thought sadly that one of them down there was mine. I looked down at the grab bar that my cuffs were chained through, then at the pilot, and then at guard sitting in the seat next to him.

The guard was staring intently off into the distance ahead of us. He spotted something that caught his attention, tapped the pilot on the shoulder, and pointed out the front canopy of the helicopter.

I looked over to where the guard was indicating, and saw a large ship that was rounding the peninsula about three miles off of the coast. It looked to be a container ship, and it had probably just left the port of Los Angeles in San Pedro.

So that was it, I was taking the proverbial 'Slow Boat to China.' That's why they held onto me in the container for so long. They had to wait for a particular ship to come into port, off-load its cargo, reload and then head back out toward the mother country. They were going to land the helicopter on the ship and drop me off for a long cruise.

Still pointing out the front canopy, the guard said something to the pilot over his head set. The pilot nodded and pushed the control stick over. We began to bank and head toward the ship. I knew I was a dead man if I they got me onto that ship and took me out of the country. I had one shot left in my life and I took it.

With all of my strength, I jerked both of my wrists and the grab bar that my hands were cuffed through broke loose on one side. I pulled the chain through just as the guard heard the commotion and turned toward me.

I was of the philosophy that there was no such thing as dirty sex or a clean fight, and so with my wrists still cuffed together, I stood up as far as I could in the back seat. I reached around the headrest and jammed my fingers deep into the pilot's eye sockets, the tips of my fingers crushing through his cornea, pupil, and all the way through the lens and the vitreous body to the back of the socket.

He shrieked in agony and pulled his hand away from the control stick and to his face. The tail rotor's blade pitch went to zero and the aircraft lost the torque to counteract the main rotor rotation. The helicopter began to spin counterclockwise.

Not understanding what was going on, the guard thrashed about in a panic. There were only seconds left before we lost complete control and so I reached down and pulled on the door handle. The door flew open and I jumped out into the darkness.

THIRTY-ONE

My body tumbled out clumsily and I was thankful I cleared the aircraft before it swung around again and smacked me with the landing skids or the tail rotor.

I had never felt that my father, a career military man, taught me much in life, but at that moment in time, desperate for things to go right, some of the words of wisdom he passed down to me came into play.

Rather than try to tuck my body into a headfirst diving position and attempt to hit the surface of the water in that position, I followed the proven technique—and military form—of crossing my arms over my chest, keeping my legs tight together, toes pointed, leaning back and going in feet first.

I had no idea how high we were when I jumped, but it seemed like it took and eternity to—

BAMMM!!!

The force seemed like an explosion at first, smacking my feet so hard it was like they had been hit by a sledgehammer. The sweatpants I was wearing shot up my legs to above my knees and into the crack of my ass. I felt my eye patch get ripped upward from my head and disappear into the water. My ears began to ring and throb from the sudden and rapid increase in pressure from the water.

I estimated that my body submerged a good fifteen to twenty feet before settling to a stop. I pressurized my mouth to equalize my ears to abate the pain in them, and then kicked my feet to push my body to the surface.

I broke through the water's surface a few long seconds later and immediately took in a huge gulp of air. I turned around in the water to try to get my bearings.

Thankfully, the ocean was reasonably calm at this time of night, and I wasn't going to be tossed around in the swells. I had just located the lights of the shore when a loud crashing sound exploded from over my right shoulder.

Instinctively and foolishly, I turned toward the sound and saw the Hughes 500—canopy first—half submerged in the water about a hundred feet away. A split second later, I heard a whizzing sound as a piece of the shattered main rotor blade went sailing over my head.

"Shit!"

That threat cleared, I treaded water and watched as the helicopter sank rapidly into the water. I couldn't tell how many bodies were inside, but I could see that only my passenger door was opened, meaning the pilot and the goon who was watching me probably never got out.

It sucked to be them, I thought to myself. But if you live by the sword, you must be ready to die by it too.

I watched as the still spinning tail rotor slipped beneath the surface; then I turned toward the shore and started to swim. The water was cold at this time of year, probably somewhere in the low sixties and I knew that I had to get to shore before hypothermia set in. I had no idea if I could make it or not.

But with my wrists stilled handcuffed—thankfully in front of me—I was limited in the strokes I could do. The front crawl was out, as well as the backstroke. I could attempt the breast stroke or the butterfly but I had never been good at either of them.

This left my choices at a modified version of either the dog paddle, or the sidestroke.

The dog paddle was tough going and not very productive and I found myself continually pulling my head down into the water with each pull of my arms. I rolled on my side and began to sidestroke.

An old swim instructor once told me that the sidestroke was a survival stroke and that if done correctly, could be performed for hours on end. I didn't know if this theory applied to those in restraints or not, but I figured if Houdini could do it, I might as well give it the old college try.

I swam for what seemed like five minutes before stopping to take a gander of my position, shivering as I did so. It appeared to me that I was making some headway and the thought buoyed me to continue on, hopefully before I began to lose strength as my body's core temperature dropped.

In another five minutes or so, I felt the faint sensation of wave action working to push my body toward the shore. This was a welcomed feeling as the west facing beaches were notorious for rip currents that trapped swimmers in an endless battle against the forces of nature, and where nature typically won. In my compromised physical state, I hoped and prayed that I wouldn't find myself in that situation.

As I soldiered on, the pulse of the swells pushing me toward shore got stronger and stronger. I craned my neck and saw that I was only about one hundred feet or so from the shore. My breathing was already becoming labored, and I knew that I was entering the first stages of exhaustion and hypothermia. My hands and feet were beginning to go numb and my teeth were chattering.

I doubled up on my stroke just as a small swell, no more than a foot and a half high, caught me and let me ride it ten or so feet toward the water's edge.

It petered out after a bit, and I continued swimming. I was in the middle of a stroke and sucking in a big breath of air as a larger swell snuck up behind me and came crashing down on me, submerging me under the water.

I inhaled a mouthful of water and when I broke the surface again, began coughing. I had barely gotten it out, and was trying to catch another breath when another wave broke over me, submerging me again.

The only good news to this was that in all its brutality and malevolence, the waves were in fact, pushing me closer to my goal.

When I popped back up again, I saw that I was only seventy feet from the water's edge. At this point, I thought I might be able to stand and walk in the rest of the way. I adjusted my body and stood up. I was in five or so feet of water and was submerged to my upper chest. My feet were so numb I couldn't feel the sand beneath them. I was shivering and weak and my legs were wobbly from swimming, but I summoned the energy to starting walking in.

Splash!!

Besides rip currents, unseen holes that dotted the area close to shore were another common hazard that clamed lives every year.

I had inadvertently stepped into one and sank in over my head. I pulled myself out of it using a dog paddle motion and swam a few feet to where I thought I had cleared it. I stood up again, walked a few feet and dropped into another hole.

Shit! I was within spitting distance of the water's edge, and yet I couldn't stand and walk the rest of the way! My lungs were burning, my legs and arms were killing me, and I was freezing and exhausted. But I had no choice at this point and wasn't about to come so far just to die a few feet from shore. I pulled myself out of the hole once again and resolved to make it the rest of the way.

I rolled over onto my side once more and continued with my half-assed sidestroke.

Only when I felt the solid feel of sand on the side of my body did I stop stroking. Rolling over onto my hands and knees, I crawled on my hands and knees out of the surf like some primeval creature from the slime. Then I collapsed on the beach.

I had escaped.

THIRTY-TWO

I laid there for a long time on the sand, shivering and catching my breath. I took stock of my situation.

I had no idea where I was, other than that I was on one of the three beaches in the South Bay area. Tiffany and I lived in the furthest north of these communities in Manhattan Beach, and hoped that I had somehow landed close to home.

I pulled my head up and tried to get my bearings. To the right of me was one long concrete pier with single structure on the end, ditto to the left. These landmarks told me that I had come ashore somewhere between the Hermosa and Manhattan Beach Piers, respectively. This put me at about a mile or so south of our home on The Strand. I stood up wobbly, pulled the legs of my sweatpants down, and started to walk home.

I had only walked a dozen or so steps before I began shaking uncontrollably.

I realized that time was of the essence, and exhausted as I was, I had to get home and warm up as soon as possible. I began to jog.

Staying on the wet sand to avoid detection, I reached the Manhattan Beach Pier a short time later, passed underneath it, and then jogged a short distance towards where I thought I would be perpendicular to our house.

I turned to the right and began plodding over the dry sand toward the houses. I was so exhausted and cold that the going was extra tough in the dry sand and I fell several times before reaching my destination.

Finally, I stepped off of the sand onto the familiar concrete of The Strand and tried to get my bearings. I knew my neighbor's houses by sight, but by now I was so weakened and disoriented, I couldn't remember if they were to the south or to the north of me.

As I stood looking and trying to get my bearings, a homeless man staggered up close by and stopped in his tracks. He took one look at me; handcuffed, soaking wet, coated with sand, and with my empty eye socket peering grotesquely at him and proclaimed, "What the fuck?"

I didn't wait around for him to figure it out and turned in the direction my addled mind thought my abode laid. Thankfully, I had turned the right direction and I was only five houses away.

I turned down the side of the house and went to the rear entrance and once there, began to push the keys on the door lock. I was shivering so much and my hands were so numb, that I had to steady one hand with another just to punch the buttons. At this point, I was just thankful I remembered the code.

The lock clicked open and I stepped inside and raced toward the bathroom and into the shower.

THIRTY-THREE

I stood under the hot water for either ten minutes or ten days, I didn't know which. I only knew that it was one of the most welcome sensations I had felt in my lifetime.

After my shivering had abated, and I felt my extremities began to burn and tingle as the blood returned to them, I exited the shower and walked dripping wet through the house to my office.

I pulled open the door to a closet that I kept my equipment in it and found a set of handcuff keys. I unlocked the cuffs, tossed them on the floor and stripped off my wet clothes. I toweled off and changed into some dry duds and then sat down at my desk to contemplate my next move.

First of all, I realized that I had no idea for sure what day or time it was. If I was going to put any sort of plan into motion to try to save McCormick or Dortell, then I had to at least know if I was too late.

I turned on my computer and while it was booting up, decided that I would probably need another cell phone at some point as well.

I took the elevator downstairs and once I had reached ground level, punched in the code to have it head to the second floor while opening the door on the first floor. I opened the hatch to the safe room and climbed down the same steps that Tiffany had descended several days ago. The motion sensor activated and the light came on. I grabbed the remaining Blackphone, switched it on, and headed back upstairs.

I had just reached my office door when the phone startled me with a shrill ring. I looked down at the display; it was Tiffany calling. I hit the soft key to answer.

Before I could even get the phone to my ear, Tiffany cried out, “Jack! Oh my God Jack you’re okay!”

“Yeah baby,” I reassured her. “I’m a little worse for wear, but I’m alive—I think.”

“I knew it!” she cried emphatically. “I knew you would make it.”

“Thanks for the vote of confidence,” I said, and then added. “But how did you know to call, and to this number?”

“I saw you on the security cameras,” she explained. “When you first came in, when you got into the shower, and when you went down into the safe room. I was hoping you’d grab the phone so I could call.”

“Well I’m glad I did too,” I said.

“Can I come home, Jack?” She pleaded. “I missed you so much.”

I pondered my situation and realized that I had no idea how much time I had or what I could accomplish. I needed to sort things out before I let Tiffany come home.

"I'm sorry baby," I said sincerely. "I've got some things I have to take care of and some people's lives are in danger. Give me a couple of hours—at the most a day, and then you can come home and we can be in each other's arms again."

She started to sob. "Please Jack, I missed you so much."

It was tough listening to her cry, but I knew that if I had her come home, I might never save McCormick or warn Dortell about what was going on. Besides that, I still wasn't even sure if either one of us could be safe. As tough as it was, I had to stand firm.

"I'm sorry baby, I really am. But I have to tie up some things, otherwise, I don't know if either of us would be safe."

I heard her continue to cry for a few more moments and then, she sniffed, and I heard her take in a big breath of air.

"Okay," she said in a tiny voice, choked with emotion. "I'll wait till I hear from you again."

"Thank you," I said, in a voice that sounded tiny to me.

"Jack," Tiffany said. "You're going to be upset with me."

"Oh," I said, suddenly taken aback. "Why is that?"

"I know that I was supposed to call the attorney, drain the accounts, and take care of all of that stuff if you didn't contact me after seventy-two hours, but I didn't."

"Why didn't you?" I asked.

"Because I knew that you would be coming back to me," she said.

I felt my throat tighten, and I fought back tears of my own. After a few seconds, I took a deep breath to fortify myself and said, "I'm not upset with you Tiffany. In fact it the most wonderful thing you could have said to me right now. I need all the confidence boosts I can get."

We were both quiet for a long time; a comfortable silence that seemed to bind us even tighter.

"I'll let you know in a couple of hours," I said. "I promise."

"Thank you, Jack. Be safe. I love you."

"I love you," I said, and then terminated the call.

THIRTY-FOUR

I sat back down at my desk and started to set the phone down. I noticed that I didn't want to release it from my grasp and realized that I was clutching it extra hard. It was, after several long days in captivity, my lifeline to Tiffany, and I didn't want to let go of it. Still, I had work to do and so I set it on the table, display up. It told me that it was Saturday, 6:21 a.m. Hell, was it that late already?

I looked out the window and sure enough, the sky was lightening.

I thought about the significance of the time and what it meant in the big scheme of things. Was I too late to warn McCormick about the little plan Moore and company had for him?

The answer was probably and sadly, yes.

If they were in fact going to arrange a boff fest as a cover story for his demise, the deed most likely would have been done by now. I couldn't take that chance though, and had to try to find out for sure.

I pulled up the file I had built on the offensive coordinator and grabbed my phone. I dialed his cell phone number. It rang five times and went to voice mail. I hung up, wondering what that proved. The answer was nothing, really. If McCormick was still alive and heard his phone, he still might not have answered it. Like most people he was probably sick of telemarketers and robo-calls and wouldn't answer an unknown number.

I glanced at my monitor again and copied down Mrs. McCormick's cell phone number. I spoofed it into my phone and dialed again.

And again, the call didn't get picked up and it went to voice mail.

I didn't get a good feeling about this, but thought that maybe McCormick was on the road or at an early morning team meeting?

I didn't know what time the Dolphins' game was, and so I went to Yahoo Sports to check the schedule.

And there it was, big as life, a screaming headline that read; UCLB Offensive Coordinator found dead in his hotel room.

THIRTY-FIVE

I fell backward into my chair and stared at the screen. I was too late; a man was dead, and my DNA was probably all over the murder scene.

After a few seconds of anguish, I sat back up and started to skim the article. It was bereft on any details other than to say that McCormick and an unknown woman were found bludgeoned to death in his hotel room and that the police were investigating.

The crime was discovered when an assistant coach went to McCormick's room to pick him up for an early morning meeting. When the offensive coordinator didn't answer, the assistant became alarmed and contacted hotel security, who opened the door. The UCLB head coach and administration have been notified and will issue a statement shortly. Stayed tuned to Yahoo sports for all the breaking news.

I clicked the Twitter icon to follow the story and stood up to pace around my office. I thought about what I knew and didn't know at this point.

At this point, McCormick and another person were dead, and I couldn't help either of them now. But Dortell still had a dangerous device implanted in him, one that could wreak havoc on his body up to and including possible death. But would the device be activated and his body controlled today? McCormick had the tablet with the special app installed in it, but was there another tablet? Or did Chris Moore somehow abscond with it and would take over McCormick's duties today? He had revealed to me that he was heading up north to catch the game and while it was true he wouldn't be calling the plays, as a sports reporter he could certainly recognize a run when he saw it and crank up the juice on Dortell. But then again, with their offensive coordinator dead, would the Dolphins be in such a state of shock that they would decide not to play?

I checked the Twitter feed on my phone and saw that no updates had been issued yet. I was stuck in a holding pattern until I knew more. But that didn't mean I couldn't be productive.

I sat back down at my desk and pulled up the file I had on Chris Moore. Thinking he was no more than a struggling wordsmith, I had previously conducted only a cursory search on him. Now it was time to bear the magnifying glass down further. I navigated to the Emperium site and entered his name, birthdate and any other pertinent info into the search field. I saw my screen populate with everything from financial records, credit reports, arrest records and medical reports. I started digging.

Being as meticulous as I could, it took only about thirty minutes before I found what I needed. Every person has a weakness, a chink in their armor to exploit, and I had found Chris Moore's. I went again to my equipment closet and started digging through it until I found what I needed. It would be a long shot to pull off, but it was the only one I had right now.

My phone chimed that I had a new tweet in my feed. It read:

After much consideration and soul searching, the Dolphins will play today, dedicating the game to their late offensive coordinator.

I navigated from the app and dialed a private jet service to secure a flight up to the bay area.

I had a game to catch today as well.

THIRTY-SIX

The impact of the landing gear touching down on the tarmac at Oakland International Airport startled me, and I realized after a few confusing moments that I had fallen asleep during the short flight from Los Angeles.

At around $3,000 an hour, using a private jet was a pricey way to travel, but I felt that at this point, I had no other choice but to charter the aircraft for the trip up here. With the airlines booking their aircraft to capacity, finding an available seat on a commercial flight on such short notice would have been nearly impossible. And I wasn't about to fly standby and risk missing the game.

After we rolled up to the area for chartered jets to disembark, the door was opened and I grabbed the duffle bag with my equipment and went down the steps onto the tarmac. I had arranged for a car to be waiting for me upon arrival, and it sat parked just a short distance away from the plane. I would have to pay the standby rate for the jet to stay here while I went to the game, but if everything went well, I should be back in an hour or so. I didn't want to be stranded here if I needed to get out of Dodge fast.

"Be back in a couple of hours or so," I said to the pilot.

"No worries," he said, and climbed back into the fuselage of the plane.

I tossed the duffle into passenger seat of the rental, switched on the ignition, and headed north toward California Memorial Stadium in Berkley, California.

The traffic was lighter than usual on a game day heading to the stadium, but that wasn't due to lack of interest. Even though a private jet was the ultimate in travel, it still didn't mean that pilots were standing by or that other details didn't have to be worked out. After rousing a pilot and getting him to the airport, the aircraft still had to be checked out, fueled, and a flight plan had to be filed. All of this prep work put me in the air later than I wanted to be, and so therefore I was late to the game. According to my Yahoo sports feed, it was already under way with the kickoff happening just moments ago.

After arriving and parking my car, I jogged along through the few latecomers and headed toward the press entrance of the stadium, all the while hearing snippets of conversation about the still fresh murder of Ken McCormick. Some people were speaking in hushed, respectful tones, but others freely speculated about the late Offensive Coordinator's troubles with infidelity. I was sure that the events of the past evening had also heightened the sense of security around the venue and on campus, and I saw scores of uniformed officers, as well as ones I recognized as undercover, stationed about.

Just before entering the stadium, I donned a counterfeit photo vest of the type required of all photographers and pulled out my phony press pass as well as my photographer pass. In my wallet, I had a driver's license, as well as credit cards, medical insurance cards, and an AAA card all in the same name. I was sweaty and breathing hard from running.

I ran up to the press entrance with my camera swinging over my neck and held out my identification for the guard to examine.

"What quarter is it?" I practically demanded of him between pants.

"Still the first," he said absently as he studied my passes.

"Shit!" I hissed. "Any score?" I asked desperately.

"I think the Dolphins just scored," he said nonchalantly, and then added, "Your driver's license please."

I pulled out my wallet and as I went to hand it to him, "accidently" dropped it to the ground, my apparent clumsiness reinforcing the facade of the desperate press photographer late to the scene to get his photos.

"Shit!" I uttered again as I picked it up. I handed it to him just as a roar went up from the crowd inside.

He handed it back to me and then with the first hint of humanity I had seen in him, said, “I’m sure there are plenty of good shots left man. Good luck.”

I thanked him and sprinted through the tunnel that led into the stadium.

THIRTY-SEVEN

Emerging from the tunnel, I spotted Chris Moore almost immediately, standing just inside the press restraining line at the corner of the stadium.

He was as spiffy as ever, and since I last saw him, he had shed his spit infused sweater—nay, he probably burned it—and had changed into a pair of dark olive pleated slacks, a light blue oxford shirt, and a crimson bow tie.

They say that clothes make the man, but right now I was more interested in what the reporter was holding then what was adorning his body. In his hands was a small tablet that I was sure had been McCormick's.

I looked out onto the field and noted that the Dolphins had the ball on the Cal Bears' twenty-five yard line just a hundred or so feet away from us.

Studiously watching the game and alternating between his tablet, Moore didn't notice me maneuver behind and to the side of him. And even if he did see me, he wouldn't have recognized me.

My hair was now an orange red and shoulder length. I had popped a glass eye into my empty socket and added a pair of glasses to complete the mix. I was also wearing a body suit that added a considerable paunch to my otherwise trim figure.

I reached into my duffle and retrieved my specially equipped Canon EOS Rebel T6i with a 650-1300mm zoom lens. I pulled the camera up to my face and shot a few bogus shots as the Dolphins huddled and then broke.

Standing over center, the quarterback barked out the snap count and the ball was hiked. The Dolphins initiated a draw play with Dortell taking the ball and streaking up the center.

I turned the camera toward Chris Moore and zoomed in on his tablet as his finger slid the soft slide-bar towards the 80% mark.

“Shit!” I cursed under my breath. He was still experimenting on that poor kid.

The Bears defense stopped Dortell at the sixteen, and the Dolphin staff called a timeout. Both teams went to the sidelines and huddled around the assistant offensive coordinator. Dortell stayed in the game, so I figured there was a good chance that he was going to be carrying the ball on the next play into the end zone.

Through my camera viewfinder, I saw Chris Moore grinning like a kid with a new toy. He was having fun playing God, but I was just about to ruin his Christmas.

I reached down into my pocket, pulled out my new Blackphone and dialed him. I wanted to make sure he knew who it was from though, and so I spoofed the old cell number I had given him into the outgoing call.

I was wearing a Bluetooth enabled throat mic with a wireless earpiece, and as soon as I saw the call dialing, I slipped the phone back into my pocket, and brought the camera up to my face, to hide my mouth.

Moore must have had his phone synched to tablet, because when it started to ring, he looked down to the tablet display with a mixture of shock and horror. He pulled the phone out of his holster and shakily held it to the side of his face.

“Hello,” he said nervously.

“Hi Chris,” I said. “Didn’t expect to be hearing my voice again, did you?”

I swung my body so that the camera was ostensibly looking out onto the field, but I zoomed out so that I could still see him in the frame. What I saw was a frightened man, desperately searching about and trying to spot me amongst the crowd of tens of thousands.

In the meantime, the two teams had just retaken the field and had lined up.

"Oh, I'm here Chris," I said. "Enjoying the game just like you."

"How…how did you…" he stammered, no longer looking at his tablet or at the action on the field.

"Oh yeah, you probably heard that the helicopter didn't make it to the ship and figured it must have must have crashed. Yeah, accidents happen all the time, and all aboard perished—except for me."

I swung the camera back around, zoomed in and aimed the Canon directly at Moore's neck, between his collar and his hairline.

In the background I could hear the snap count being called and then the crush of bodies as the ball was hiked. All eyes, except for mine and Moore's, were trained on the action on the field.

"So, how's about you go keep your partners in crime company?" I said as I flipped open the cover to a secondary switch on my camera, and depressed the button.

Just below the long telephoto lens of the camera was a short, rifled barrel. A C02 cartridge inside the camera released its pressure and propelled a small metal dart with a hypodermic needle on the end down the barrel, and towards Moore's neck.

I saw the dart hit him just a split-second later. His hand instinctively went up to his neck just as the crowd roared when the Dolphins put up another score.

Moore couldn't have cared less about the game, or Dortell, or his employers at that moment, and he desperately pulled the dart out from his neck. By then, however, it was too late. The heavily concentrated bee venom had already entered his system and would soon begin doing its magic.

For all his good looks, charming personality, and fancy wardrobe sense, Chris Moore had one very dangerous fault: he was highly allergic to bee stings.

As the crowd continued to carry on about the latest score, I walked slowly toward Moore, who was now starting to twist and writhe as his windpipe began to constrict and cut off his air supply. He dropped his phone and the tablet onto the field and his hands were clutching in a panic at his neck.

I walked up casually to him and he turned to face me. Already his eyes were bulging out and his face had begun to swell up.

"Yeah, I know about your allergy to bee stings," I said nonchalantly.

I reached into my pocket and pulled out an Epinephrine Auto-Injector, otherwise known as an e*pi pen* that I dropped into his pocket.

"And I also know that have a prescription for one of these, but never carry it with you," I continued. "Probably figure it was going to wrinkle your fancy pants or something."

Moore tried to speak but his tongue had swollen so much it was unintelligible. His face was turning blue, and a second later, he collapsed onto the artificial turf.

I leaned over him and put on a show that I was trying to help him and administer first aid. In reality, I pulled the dart from his hand and delivered the last words he would ever hear.

"But don't worry Chris, it's just like we're turbocharging your body."

A couple of EMTs came running up just then.

“What happened?” the first of the EMTs yelled out above the crowd noise.

“I don’t know,” I said. “I think he got stung by a bee. He was clutching at his neck and then he couldn’t breathe and he collapsed.”

“Sir, sir, can you hear us?” the second EMT asked.

Moore couldn’t answer and was looking straight at me with his bulging eyes.

“He was clutching at his pocket,” I offered. “Maybe he has some medicine.”

One of the EMTs reached into Moore’s pocket and pulled out the auto-injector I had placed in there. With practiced deftness, he popped the cap, slid out the injector, took aim and drove it into Moore’s thigh, unknowingly injecting a lethal dose of pure adrenaline into his body and sealing the former reporter’s fate.

By now a stretcher had been brought over by a couple of more medical personnel. I took the opportunity during all of the commotion to pick up Moore’s tablet, drop it into my duffle and slip away. I walked off the field as I heard another roar erupt from the crowd, but I didn't look back.

I strode out through the same tunnel I had entered just moments earlier and headed towards the security checkpoint.

The same guard was on duty and was playing around with his phone. When he saw me, he looked up in surprise.

"What happened?" he said.

"Mother-fuckers fired me," I said. "Just for missing the first play of the game."

"That sucks," he said.

"Yeah, but I did get the one good shot I was hoping for," I said, before continuing on.

THIRTY-EIGHT

"That's bullshit!" Dortell Williams shouted.

"Dortell!" his grandfather admonished in his deep baritone. "No cursing, not in our house."

I was standing in the living room of Dortell's grandparents. It was close to two o'clock and they had finished their church services and were home for the day. The two men had shed their suit coats and loosened their ties and Mrs. Williams was setting their table for Sunday dinner. I could smell the fragrant aroma of sweet potatoes, green beans, and pork roast permeating throughout the house.

"Sorry Grandpa," Dortell said sheepishly. He pointed up at me in an accusatory manner. "But you don't know what he told…"

I cut him off.

"Listen Dortell," I said. "I knew that you wouldn't believe me, so I want to prove it to you."

I pulled out McCormick's old tablet and pressed the switch to turn it on.

As it was booting up, I said. "Do you recognize this, Dortell? It's McCormick's tablet."

He shrugged. "It could be," he said. "But then it could be any tablet. You can get one anywhere."

Yep, I was going to have to prove it to him alright.

"Oh, it's not just any tablet," I said as I launched the app for the adrenal gland stimulator. "And I'm going to prove it to you now."

"I moved the slide bar over to twenty percent and a moment later, Dortell's body stiffened and shook a little bit.

"You feel that?" I asked.

"I…I feel kind of funny," Dortell admitted. "Kind of like I feel in a game."

"Right," I said. "Now do me a favor, get down and give me thirty pushups—as fast as you can."

"What?" he cried incredulously.

"Just do it, Dortell," his grandfather said genially. "Let's just see what the gentleman has here."

The UCLB running back nodded, and assumed the position on the living room floor. Mechanically he started to crank out pushups as only a young man could.

I tilted the tablet display so that the elder Williams could see it and then slid the bar over to eighty-nine percent. Almost instantly, Dortell's speed increased exponentially. He began doing pushups almost faster than we could count.

I moved the slider back to zero and Dortell collapsed on the floor.

He started to sniffle and put his hands over his eyes.

"I'm sorry, Grandpa," he said in a choked voice. "I didn't know I was cheating. I feel so bad."

"It's not your fault, Dortell," I reassured him. "You had no way of knowing, and were just in the wrong place at the wrong time. No one can blame you. In fact, once we get this device out of you, we're going to send it to the International Olympic Committee so that they can be made aware of it. With them on the lookout, they can test and hopefully prevent it from ever being used again. You probably have saved the lives of numerous athletes.

Dortell rolled over on his side then and pulled his hands away from his face. His eyes were red and his cheeks were wet with tears.

"Really?" he asked hopefully.

"Yes," I said. "Really. Without knowing it, you're going to be a hero."

He nodded, and then added sadly, "But just not out on the football field, right?"

"Time will tell, but at least you can play knowing in your heart that it's an honest effort."

"And that's what the Lord would want, Dortell," his grandfather added.

I nodded to reaffirm the statement. The poor kid had just been handed a bombshell, and needed all the support he could get.

"I'll start making the arrangements for you to have the device removed, Dortell," I said. "We have access to special surgeons that can do this work without any knowledge of it showing up on your medical history."

"So no one will ever know?" he suggested.

"Right, no one will ever know, except for us in this room."

"And God," Mr. Williams added.

"Yes," I said. "And God."

Dortell bolted to his feet and hugged me.

"Thank you," he said.

"You're very welcome," I said, as we embraced for few moments.

Dortell broke it off after a short time and I reached over to shake his grandfather's hand.

"And thank you, sir," I said, "For allowing me into your home. And now, I'll leave you folks to your Sunday dinner."

I stated to turn to leave.

"Oh no," the elder Williams said, putting a firm hand on my shoulder. He turned in the direction of the kitchen.

"Leona," he called out, "Set another plate."

Then he turned back to me and smiled.

"We never let a person leave this house hungry," he said firmly. "And we aren't gonna start now."

It was delicious.

EPILOGUE

Chris Moore was pronounced dead on arrival at the Alta Bates Summit Medical Center. The cause of death was attributed to a severe case of anaphylactic shock, secondary to a bee sting. As it was a naturally produced substance and would dissipate in his body after a short time, the toxicology report made no mention of the excess of adrenaline in his body injected via the epi pen by the EMT's that evening.

Since we're talking death, not surprisingly, the pilot and guard never survived the helicopter crash that I orchestrated that fateful evening. Additionally, as the aircraft went down in an area not generally explored by divers, the wreckage was not discovered and might never be found.

So that he wouldn't have to miss any games, Dortell finished the season before having surgery to remove the device. That was fine with me as it took a quite a bit of coordination on my end to pull it off. The device and a copy of the program loaded into a fresh tablet were sent anonymously to the International Olympic Committee along with a narrative about how it worked and who was behind it. The Chinese government denied the allegations emphatically.

Without the boost of adrenaline during his play on the field, Dortell's performance suffered somewhat, but he still ended up scoring eight touchdowns and gaining over seven hundred yards for the season, keeping his spot on the team and his scholarship intact. Although he was now just a 'good' player and might not be considered for the NFL draft, he was content with just finishing school and intended to go on to graduate school to get his doctorate in theology. He planned to go on another mission to the Philippine Islands during the summer, and wanted to dedicate his life to Christ.

I anonymously mailed the drugs that I had Kowalski buy for me to the NCAA, and dropped Jerry's name to them as well as to UCLB and the DEA. In addition to that, I also sent a nice little note to the IRS, detailing Mr. Pine's bogus income stream. Besides all of the heat he was going to feel for dealing performance enhancing drugs to college athletes, the erstwhile Juice-Man would soon find himself the recipient of an investigation into his tax returns that was so deep, it would feel like the financial equivalent of a colonoscopy.

And as for myself, other than tying up the aforementioned loose ends, I've been too busy and preoccupied to worry much about the machinations of others, past or future. Tiffany moved back home and we are thankfully together again, but just for how long is the question. This has nothing to do with any acrimony between us or a degradation of our relationship, which for the record, is as strong as ever. It's just the pesky little matter of the Berkley Police Department, who, three and a half weeks after the murder of Ken McCormick and his female companion, issued a warrant for my arrest.

THE END

"Let the sea roar, and the fullness thereof; the world, and they that dwell therein." PSALM 98:7

SWEPT AWAY

By

Chris Moore

3:37 PM: SAN FRANCISCO, CALIFORNIA

It struck with ample warning. The colossal wave of seawater surged through the meandering, rush hour streets of downtown San Francisco, lugging cars and trolleys through the city like children's toys.

Mother Nature was reclaiming the coastal metropolis for herself, clawing at the compact city with giant, avenging hands that raked parts of San Francisco into the sea and, with malicious cruelty, reached back into the town for more.

Wave after enormous wave blitzed the hapless coast as far inland as two miles, and the receding seawater, as tall as two-storied houses, foamed and fizzled like gallons of spilled soda—dragging people, pets and debris out into the open sea. Others clinged to anything they could to keep from being swept away.

EARLIER THAT DAY: THE ALASKAN COAST

The Alaskan air was crisp; the sky, cloudless and the sun shone with noon like radiance. The sea's swells licked and lapped the coastal shores like playful puppies, while sullied gulls squawked and glided in tight, hungry circles above the frigid waters.

The coast was more cliff than beach; more snow than sand, and the awaiting sunset—the Northern Lights—would eventually cast the entire Alaskan sky in swirling rainbows that danced like sweltering flames.

***

Three miles beneath the surface calm, in the black, abysmal depths along the Continental Shelf, the earth ripped and then shook—sloshing enough seawater to fill the Great Lakes twice, and sending it surging through the Pacific Ocean like a trampling herd of Bison.

***

9:03 AM: 2000 MILES AWAY, NEW ALCATRAZ STATE PRISON, SAN FRANCISCO BAY

On a small, rocky island off the coast of San Francisco, a speckled seagull nipped greedily at a half-eaten halibut outside a razor wire fence surrounding California's newest prison for women.

Alcatraz, the infamous penitentiary that once housed notorious prisoners like Al Capone and Machine Gun Kelly, was a ghost of its former self. The State had purchased the landmark site, demolished the old federal prison known as 'The Rock' and had built a state of the art prison complex where the old one once stood, renaming it 'New Alcatraz'. It was heralded, like Alcatraz, to be escape proof and was designed to forever incarcerate the State's most dangerous women.

'The Iron Rock' was its new moniker and from the air, it looked like a steel landing platform with five Millennium Falcons parked evenly in a half circle, that—by design—formed a dirt courtyard where inmates could exercise. At times of unrest, prison guards dressed like green storm troopers marched in ominous formation, while inmates—rebels in blue jumpsuits—desperately ran for cover.

At times of peace, on mornings of thick, coastal fog, New Alcatraz looked like an abandoned space settlement drifting on an asteroid through clouds of nebula in a sea of deep blue space.

***

Inside, ten inmates and four staff members gathered in a small classroom in the prison's administration building.

"I can't do it anymore," cried Whining Wanda, an aging convict who was battling breast cancer and was serving her thirty-fifth year in prison for killing her abusive husband.

"I'm sick of doing time. I'm sick of being sick," she rambled on. "I can't do this anymore—I just can't. I wish I…" a small voice quickly interjected from across the room.

"Don't say it," the voice pleaded. "Please, don't say it."

Whining Wanda nodded quietly, rocking back and forth in a metal folding chair that faced the group; her knees together, her hands trembling.

"Why," Judgmental Judy, the group's critic demanded. Severe fault finding, a symptom of Post-Traumatic Stress Disorder, was what led Judgmental Judy to kill a woman in a bar fight several years ago. Even in her late sixties, she was strong and had a penchant for fighting, a trait she inherited from the time she served honorably in a M.A.S.H. unit during the Vietnam War. Now, in a twist of fate, she found herself battling a cancer that was as pugnacious and judgmental as she was.

"Why what," retorted Freedom Florence, her tone challenging, tension building between the two. Freedom Florence was the consummate protector of the group and was quick to run to the aid of the weak. No one knew what terrible deed she had committed to end up in prison, but it didn't matter. She had earned the respect and admiration of those around her, except for a few.

"Why shouldn't she say it?" replied Judgmental Judy, clearly annoyed. "Why should she keep it all bottled up inside of her? It's how most of us feel anyway, so why shouldn't she say it?"

Joyful Jenny, the one who had asked Whining Wanda not to say it, looked over at Freedom Florence with wide, curious, expecting eyes. At four-feet-six, Joyful Jenny was the smallest of the group members and was just ten years old. She was one of three special child visitors in the group: Jealous Jessie, her slightly taller twin and Brave Brittany, her best friend in the whole wide world. All of them were fighting deadly cancers and all of them were losing the battle, their petite bald heads evidence of failed radiation treatments and chemotherapies.

Their visits were part of a yearlong pilot program dubbed, 'Women For Honor' that sought to bring sick children together with sick prisoners with the far away hope of unearthing the precious oil of inner healing.

It took the Cancer Institute and prison administrators seven years to start the program, and after only one year of weekly meetings, the program was now in jeopardy. The shifting political climate on crime gave prison management the excuse they needed to shut it all down: the group's progress was inconclusive and fell suspiciously short of the expectations set by prison officials, not to mention the safety of the children. Still, like devoted protesters of the Civil Rights movement, the group met every single week.

"Because they're children. That's why," Freedom Florence answered emphatically, looking at the three girls sitting together. Her gaze softened, lingering on Joyful Jenny for just a moment longer than the others. Perhaps it was because Joyful Jenny was so little and wearing mechanical leg braces that made her seem more vulnerable than the other two, or maybe it was that she reminded her so much of her own daughter; a daughter from whom she had been exiled for the past twenty years.

Freedom Florence turned away, emotions creeping in. Children, she thought, innocent children who had been unfairly afflicted with the world's most deadly disease and for what? To what end? She would gladly sacrifice herself and bear all of their illnesses, giving them all a chance to live long, healthy, happy lives. After all, she was guilty—her life marred forever by a single, horrible act. Then, that voice, that small voice caught her attention, bringing her out of her self-reproaching inner soliloquy.

"We shouldn't…" Joyful Jenny began, speaking so softly that she had to clear her throat and start again.

"We shouldn't say it, because it's not true."

"Why don't you think it's true, Jenny?" This time it was the prison's psychiatrist, Dr. Ann. The group insisted on calling the doctor by her adjective name, Analytical Ann, but she refused to be addressed that way. "It's inappropriate," she would say.

Everybody in the group was required to have an adjective name—an alliterative name that combines an adjective that describes a personality trait with a first name.

"What do you mean it's not true, Jenny," the doctor repeated.

Joyful Jenny looked at Whining Wanda with round, discerning eyes.

"It's not true because she wants to live."

Whining Wanda nodded greedily, feasting on Joyful Jenny's truth like a famished nomad.

"She wants," Joyful Jenny continued, "what we all so desperately want: hope. The doctors tell me that I won't be here come Christmas." Joyful Jenny turned and looked solemnly at Healing Harriet, the oncologist from the institute who sat there with tears welling in her eyes.

"They tell me that my courage is greater than my strength. But I would rather them tell me that I am as strong as I am courageous, because through the strength of hope and love, I know we can all be healed."

Joyful Jenny redirected her gaze at Whining Wanda, her eyes deep and compassionate.

"You are immeasurable love, Wanda. Please don't let life's short-lived miseries take that gift away from you."

Gloomy Gloria, a young, reticent prisoner who resembled a chubby Lucille Ball, covered her mouth and wiped her eyes, hiding tears and her astonishment at Joyful Jenny's insightful and compassionate answer.

Gloomy Gloria was a victim of pancreatic cancer. She was also a murderer by accomplice. During a home invasion robbery, her partner in crime senselessly murdered one of the occupants—the husband— and although she hadn't killed anyone, the State saw to it that she shared equally in the guilt and in a lifetime of punishment.

Gloomy Gloria was a manic and a depressant whose life was a dichotomy of two stories. Her right arm, decorated with artful tattoos, heralded her as a fighter, but her left arm, riddled with grizzly scars, accused her of being a quitter.

"I love your answer, Jenny," chimed Helpful Hanna, one of the two counselors from the institute who was also a successful writer who had published a best-selling novel entitled, *One Eyed Jackie*, "but what about when bad things happen to you and you feel sad like Whining Wanda?"

Joyful Jenny's expression changed. Her eyes grew sad, her lips pursed in a way that only a child could purse them, and her rosy cheeks grew rosier.

"To me, sickness and the awful things that happen are not lifelong condemnations but are dreams that remind me that life is about healing and forgiveness. It makes me want to embrace life, not to let go of it."

The group was pin drop silent. It was an incredibly simple answer, uncomplicated by the hamartia of grown-up reasoning.

***

9:47 AM: D-BLOCK, NEW ALCATRAZ PRISON

In the main living quarters of the prison, inmates milled about. Some playing cards, others just standing around, all of them wearing blue jumpsuits with the words, 'CDCR PRISONER' stenciled on the back of their uniforms in large, yellow lettering.

This group of prisoners lived in one of the five buildings that looked like a Millennium Falcon; a two-story concrete structure that curved in a half circle at the back and tapered to a V-shape point at the front. Small, two person cells lined the rear, rounded portion of the unit and extended two hundred seventy degrees toward the guard's station at the front, giving the sentries a clear, unobstructed view of all fifty cells.

A second story, inner observation tower was built into the front of the building and was posted by an armed guard who could shoot any target inside or outside of the unit. The cavernous space inside the building was referred to as the 'dayroom', where inmates regularly assembled for recreational activities.

A group of inmates had gathered to watch a recorded episode of *Orange is the New Black* on a wall–mounted television in the dayroom. They laughed and made crude comments. Ten minutes into the show, a breaking news banner flashed across the screen. A news anchor urgently reported the breaking headline.

"A nine-point-six earthquake was registered off the coast of Alaska. The epicenter was thousands of feet beneath the ocean. Tsunami warnings have been issued for Pacific coastal areas and are to remain in effect for the next twenty-four hours. We'll have more on this late-breaking event."

Dozens more curious inmates gathered to watch. A young, tattooed gang member with braids called Scrappy asked, "Hey, are we part of the coastal areas?"

Several prisoners turned with scowls on their faces that read, "What are you, stupid? Yeah, we're part of the coastal areas. Duh!" Yet, for all of their collective brilliance, not one of them realized the horrible catastrophe that was heading their way.

The television suddenly went black and a collective 'aw' rose from the group of inmates. An awkward silence followed. Static crackled over the Public Address system and a guard's voice commanded all the inmates to return to their cells.

The inmates were complying with the command until a terrifying realization crashed into Scrappy like a massive wave. "Hey," Scrappy shouted, "the tidal wave is coming this way!"

Tidal wave was a misnomer. Most people imagine a tidal wave as a towering wave that sweeps inland and causes a great loss of life. In truth, tidal waves are often small, harmless waves that fluctuate with tidal conditions, hence the name tidal wave.

Tsunami—Japanese for 'harbor wave'—on the other hand, is a giant wave spawned by an undersea earthquake or other event. In the open ocean it may take the form of successive waves, traveling up to five hundred miles per hour and at a deceptive height of only three feet. As it approaches the coastal shallows, tsunamis slow down and grow to enormous heights and become the gargantuan wall of water depicted in Hollywood movies.

Mental lightbulbs, one by one, began flickering on in the rest of the prisoners. Someone yelled, "They're gonna lock us all up and leave us here to die!"

More commands were given for the inmates to lock up. More inmates joined the uproar. Then, all hell broke loose.

***

10:13 AM: ADMINISTRATION BUILDING

Freedom Florence broke the silence. "I had a dream last night."

"What kind of dream," Whining Wanda asked.

"I was falling, but I wasn't afraid. Someone was holding my hand on the way down. It seemed like I was falling forever, then I landed softly on a blue cloud."

She looked around to see the group's reaction, but there was none.

She went on. "I don't know what it all means, but in my dream, I felt truly free for the first time in my life. I mean really free."

Judgmental Judy rolled her eyes.

"Love is knocking on your door," Joyful Jenny responded. "Answer it and you will find the love that cast out fear and it will set you on a soft eternal cloud of freedom and truth."

Judgmental Judy had endured enough. "Stop it with the philosophical BS. The truth is that we're all locked up doing life, we're all sick and we're all going to die in this miserable rat hole. And don't think for a minute…"

The prison's alarm started blaring. Something was wrong.

The doctor and both counselors stood up, checking outside the room for signs of a disturbance.

Fearful Frances began fidgeting in her chair, her hands sweating.

"Does anyone have an Oreo cookie," she asked weakly.

The group shook their heads, unaffected by her unusual request. They understood her peculiar reaction. Whenever Fearful Frances became scared, she would always ask for the same thing: an Oreo cookie. Occasionally, she would get one but most of the time she was forced to deal with her fear without one. Either way, it was just Fearful Frances' strange, almost humorous, way of coping with her own trepidation.

An ear-piercing scream came from down the hallway, just outside the room. Everyone jumped.

Freedom Florence scurried over to Joyful Jenny and knelt beside her.

The doctor locked the door and returned to the group.

"Look, something's going on," Dr. Ann began. "We're going to stay put until we know what's going on or until we get instructions. Okay?"

The group nodded.

Outside, the staccato sound of automatic gunfire could be heard and the building rattled under the deafening booms of flash grenades. The acrid smell of pepper spray began seeping into the room.

Several group members began to cough, their eyes watering under the stingy effects of loose mace.

A cacophony of sounds was taking place in the hallway just outside the room. Screams and shouts, commands and orders, and none of it made any sense. Then, the dreadful sound of multiple struggles—grunts and shrieks—and soon after, gunfire.

Brave Brittany and Fearful Frances began sobbing hysterically. Others strained to contain their fright.

Dr. Ann got on her cell phone. She spoke and hung up.

Freedom Florence gathered the children into her arms to form a tight circle.

The door shook, its knob rattled and a fist pounded desperately for entry.

There were more shouts, more struggles and more gunfire. The door stopped clattering and an eerie silence followed.

Everyone in the room was afraid to move. Freedom Florence quietly ushered the children into the safest corner of the room, away from any sudden breach of the door. The rest of the group followed.

The room that held them was windowless, a concrete bunker buried deep inside the prison's command center where, like a bomb shelter, they could hear the muffled explosions of warfare.

They sat on the floor in a semicircle looking like a battered group of survivors from a plane crash and for the first thirty minutes no one said a word. They just listened to the carnage taking place outside the walls.

The group began to make small talk. Their talk evolved into laughter and their laughter turned into sadness. Soon their sadness became resentment;

their resentment turned into anger and anger turned into shouting and fighting. Like a vicious cycle, crying and forgiveness came last and then it started all over again. All of it was an attempt to distract themselves from the insanity waiting just beyond the walls. But the war on the other side would not be ignored.

The sound of exploding grenades and screams jolted the group back into silence.

It was difficult to imagine that guards had lost control of the prison, but the screech of rubber soles against a polished floor—the sound of a lone inmate skipping down the ruinous hallway, shouting the lyrics of songs from the sixties and rapping the walls with a guard's baton—was sufficient proof that the unthinkable had happened.

It was five long, tortuous hours before Dr. Ann's cell phone rang. She listened, nodded and hung up.

Dr. Ann turned and looked anxiously at the door. Six times previously, someone had tried desperately to enter. The last time was over an hour ago.

Dr. Ann turned to the group, their eyes pleading for an answer.

"There's a tsunami headed toward the west coast," she began. "Evacuations have been ordered for all coastal cities but widespread panic has made it almost impossible. The inmates at the prison have risen up…"

"Damn right!" Judgmental Judy interjected.

"We have to make our way to the roof where we'll be safe and can wait for help," Dr. Ann finished.

"There's a stairwell just down the hall that accesses the roof," spouted Silly Sandra. They all agreed to stay together and made their way to the door.

They huddled together, crouching through the smoky corridor where bodies of inmates and guards littered the floor. Shrieking alarms blared incessantly and rapid fire gunshots could be heard in the distance. Somewhere, a roar of inmates erupted with more crackle of gunfire.

They reached the stairwell to the roof.

Joyful Jenny wrapped her arms around Freedom Florence's neck, her crippled legs dangling like loose shoestrings over Freedom Florence's straining arms.

Three flights of stairs were all that stood between them and the roof, where they would be safe from the violence and they would wait for help. Joyful Jenny wheezed and coughed erratically and Freedom Florence quickly covered her mouth with a T-shirt.

"Hang in there, baby," Freedom Florence urged.

They had reached the roof and a helicopter could be heard whirring in the distance. They stood on the rooftop, wildly waving their arms in the air.

The aircraft was a police helicopter and several heavily armed SWAT officers were perched like hawks on both sides of the chopper.

As they made their approach, the officers pointed at the children and waved everyone else away. Freedom Florence gently laid Joyful Jenny on the ground and stepped away.

"Don't leave me, Florence," Joyful Jenny begged.

"I have to go, baby, but I'll see you again. I promise."

"Promise," Joyful Jenny asked.

Freedom Florence nodded with tears in her eyes, her clothes flailing in the chopper's draft.

The helicopter landed and the SWAT team dismounted, rifles pointed. They grabbed the children and ushered the counselors and doctors onto the waiting chopper. Freedom Florence took a step forward. An officer pointed his weapon at her head.

"Get down! Get down, now!"

Freedom Florence and the rest of the inmates got on their knees, hand behind their heads.

The SWAT team quickly retreated to the helicopter, guns still pointed. The lifting chopper rose haphazardly into the air and then banked up and away.

Joyful Jenny looked down at the roof. She could see the approaching wave in the distance stalking the prison like a giant crocodile. She let out a bloodcurdling scream that went unheard, drowned out by the popping rotor blades.

Joyful Jenny watched in horror as the massive wave hit the prison with a roar. Freedom Florence was still on the rooftop, kneeling with outstretched arms when the wave swallowed her pleading body and the entire prison in one enormous bite.

Everything had been swept away.

***

ONE YEAR LATER—SOMEWHERE IN THE PACIFIC

The sun hung in a velvety, azure sky like a glittering diamond, beaming warm sunrays on a tiny island that was rich in lush, mountainous foliage. Brisk gales wafted the salty scent of ocean through the island's thick, green flora while streams of fresh water coalesced at a cliff's edge and spilled over the side into a blue lagoon thirty feet below.

A couple stood at the cliff's edge, their hands linked together like connecting cables and their eyes lost in each other's dreamy gaze.

"I now pronounce you united in holy matrimony," a voice said solemnly.

Tears flowed down Freedom Florence's face, her gown fluttering in the wind.

She looked from her soulmate to the two people standing next to her and stifled an urge to cry, letting out instead a tearful chuckle. Her daughter, Florina, smiled and reached out to her for a hug.

Her dream had finally come true.

Natives serenaded the couple's union with hand drums that rapped a catchy, Caribbean tune.

"Three," a voice began counting down.

Freedom Florence looked at the bright, orange life vest strapped to her chest. She didn't know how to swim, but that was okay. She had never felt safer in all her life.

"Two."

The couple turned and faced one another, reuniting their dreamy gaze. The drumbeat gradually became louder, rising into a crescendo.

"One."

Freedom Florence closed her eyes, whispered to herself and with her mate, leapt off the edge of the waterfall, descending toward the lagoon below.

Her whispers turned into talk as she fell over the side. She had been reciting the adjective names of the unforgettable friends that had, for so long, touched her life—a tribute to their lives, their struggles and their search for freedom.

"Whining Wanda, Gloomy Gloria, Silly Sandra, Loveable Linda, Insightful Isabel, Helpful Hanna, Analytical Ann, Fearful Frances, Angry Alexis, Dramatic Dorothy, Brave Brittany, Jealous Jessie…"

She opened her eyes, still falling; the thoughts about the loss of her friends falling with her and whispered the last of the endearing names: Joyful Jenny, who was standing over the edge of the cliff with Florina, watching her descend and splash into the water below.

***

"The LORD on high is mightier than the noise of many waters, yea, than the mighty wave of the sea." PSALM 93:4

EPILOGUE

SWEPT AWAY is a fictional story that is based on the amazing things that I have seen and heard in the creative writer's workshop hosted by Christopher J. Lynch. It was a privilege to build a moving and dramatic story that conveyed a message of hope, but also incorporated elements of personal experiences from the classmates themselves.

SWEPT AWAY is both a literal and an allegorical story. In a literal sense, it is a story about a group of women and children who struggle with illness and incarceration in a prison setting, when suddenly, their lives are threatened by a catastrophic tsunami that strikes the prison. It ends with two of the characters being reunited on a tropical island and living out their dreams.

Allegorically, it is a story that symbolizes the deeper truths of the criminal justice system and the inextinguishable human drive to persevere and discover hope.

New Alcatraz represents not just a single prison, but an entire criminal justice system built on a rock of old, draconian precepts that seeks to incarcerate people far more than it seeks to free them, and treats the incarcerated with cruel indifference—as expendable objects—rather than irreplaceable human beings with limitless potential.

The group represents prisoners everywhere who struggle to find change and also the many facets of the human condition. Cancer is the incurable and fatal stigma placed on those who are incarcerated and upon those who attempt to help them.

The children symbolize the deep, nagging, insightful truths of our inner child. It is that part of us where forgiveness, love and compassion lie locked away in a cage of tragic experiences and can only be unlocked by the key of recognizing our own childhood innocence.

The tsunami represents 'change' and how it rumbles in the deep recesses of our being, rippling through us and sweeping us away into a new life—a life with new meaning and a new way of thinking. Like tsunamis, 'change' comes in waves, washing away old habits that we often fight to hold on to. It is something we see coming from afar, but there is little we can do to avoid it until it is right upon us and crashing into us with life's transformative power. Nothing is ever the same after a tsunami.

The tropical ending symbolizes…FREEDOM.

ABOUT THE AUTHOR

Chris Moore, whose own adjective name is Caring Chris, is an aspiring writer and a strong advocate of criminal justice reform. Chris is serving his tenth year of a life sentence under the Three Strikes Law, and in the last several years he has discovered the transformative and healing power of creative writing. His stories are often set inside a prison and are meant to enrich the lives of its readers with engaging plots, dynamic characters, profound dialogue and deep, provocative themes. Chris has helped instruct a creative writing class in prison and in his spare time, he is a barber, an athlete, a chess player and a friend who helps others rediscover their own capacity for compassion and hope.

Chris is currently incarcerated in the California State Prison at Post Office Box 4430 in Lancaster, California 93539. His prison ID number is AK6450.

About the Author

South Bay author Christopher J. Lynch has written for numerous local and national publications on a variety of topics including:

- interviewing one of the last surviving Buffalo Soldiers,

- visiting incarcerated veterans in a maximum security prison who perform fundraisers to raise money for our troops overseas,
- and telling the story of a Manhattan Beach test pilot who was the first man to survive a supersonic bailout of an aircraft,

He also authored, ***Eddie: the Life and Times of America's Preeminent Bad Boy,*** the authorized biography of the iconic child actor Ken Osmond, (Eddie Haskell from the TV series *Leave it to Beaver*).

He gives back to his community by serving as a mentor for a writing program in a maximum-security prison north of Los Angeles, as well as providing free self-publishing seminars to other writers.

When he's not writing, Christopher enjoys mountain climbing and distance cycling. He's reached the summits of Mount Whitney, Mount Kilimanjaro in Africa, as well as a trek to Mount Everest Base Camp. He once trained and led eleven blind hikers to the

summit of 10,000-ft. Mount Baldy, the highest point in Los Angeles County, and the third highest point in Southern California. A documentary film is being made of the adventure. His latest adventures were a bicycling trip of Cuba, a trip to Moscow, Russia, and witnessing the recent total solar eclipse in Idaho. He is planning a trek to Patagonia in the fall of 2018
His website is http://www.christopherjlynch.com

Also by Christopher J. Lynch

One Eyed Jack

https://www.amazon.com/One-Eyed-Jack-Christopher-Lynch/dp/1475174438/ref=asap_bc?ie=UTF8

Russian Roulette

https://www.amazon.com/Russian-Roulette-Eyed-Jack-novel/dp/0615874460/ref=asap_bc?ie=UTF8

Sin Tax

https://www.amazon.com/Sin-Tax-Eyed-Jack-Novel/dp/0990727319/ref=asap_bc?ie=UTF8

Eddie: The Life and Times of America's Preeminent Bad Boy

https://www.amazon.com/Eddie-Life-Times-Americas-Preeminent/dp/0990727300/ref=asap_bc?ie=UTF8

www.ingramcontent.com/pod-product-compliance
Lightning Source LLC
Chambersburg PA
CBHW061306170626
46817CB00001B/71

* 9 7 8 0 9 9 0 7 2 7 3 3 0 *